THE MILL HOUSE
MYSTERY

THE MILL HOUSE MYSTERY

FLORENCE WARDEN

CHAPTER I.
AN ACCIDENT

THE July sun was pouring floods of blinding, glaring light upon the town of Dourville, which, lying in a great chasm between two high white lines of cliff, and straggling under the foot of them to east and west, bears witness, in its massive castle, and in its old relics of stone buildings among the commonplace iron frames and plate-glass windows of the new, to the notable part it has taken in England's history.

The long straight road that goes northwards up through the town and out of the town, rising, at first by slow degrees, and latterly by a steep ascent, to a point from which one can look down upon town and sea, soon leaves small shops for queer old-fashioned rows of houses; and these in their turn give place to roomy old residences of greater pretension.

At the back of one of these, a sombre, plain building, roomy rather than dignified, there stretches a splendid expanse of garden and pleasaunce, where a stream runs among meadows and lawns in a direct line towards the sea.

This stream once supplied the power that worked a great paper-mill, which was the foundation of the prosperity of the Hadlow family. But three generations back, the reigning Hadlow, more enterprising than his predecessors, had speculated outside his little world, had prospered, and finally blossomed into the great philanthropist, whose magnificent endowment of certain royal charities had earned him a baronetcy.

Rich as the family had grown, the Hadlows clung to the old nest with a pertinacity which had in it something of dignity; and only the condition in which the grounds were kept, nothing in the appearance of the house itself, would have betrayed that now, under the third baronet, the place was the property of a man of great wealth.

The trees grew thickly within the high dark wall that shut the grounds in from the road. And under their shade Sir Robert Hadlow, in a light linen suit and shady planter's hat, could saunter at his ease in the heat of the day. A man of middle height, slight and almost boyish in figure, with a close-trimmed dark beard and large, mild, grey eyes, Sir Robert Hadlow, at thirty years of age, looked rather older by reason of the quiet gravity of his manners and the leisurely dignity of his movements.

A man of leisure, he had devoted himself early and enthusiastically to the study of the antiquities of the neighbourhood in which he was born; and something of the far-away look of the student softened and mellowed the expression of his eyes, and gave a certain measured dignity to his gait.

Stopping from time to time to peep between the branches of the lilac-bushes at the stream as it sparkled in the bright sunlight beyond, he was sauntering towards the house, when a succession of piercing screams, followed by the shouts of men, reached his ears from the road outside.

"Stop her!" "Look out!" "She'll be killed!"

These, among others, were the cries which came to Sir Robert's ears as he hurriedly made his way to one of the wooden doors in the high wall, and inserting into the lock his own private key, let himself through into the public street.

Looking up the road, to the left, he saw the figure of a woman, in a light dress, coming swiftly down the hill on a bicycle, of which it was evident that she had lost control. A glance to the right showed him a traction engine coming slowly up the hill with a couple of waggons trailing behind it, and the confused cries of the bystanders called his attention to the fact that it was a collision between this and the bicycle which they all feared.

Stepping forward into the road, and watching the light machine vigilantly as it came quickly down upon him, Sir Robert prepared for his rather risky attempt to save the woman from her danger. As the bicycle reached him he turned to run with it down the hill, at the same time seizing the handlebar with so much dexterity that he neither stopped the machine nor threw off its rider.

The woman was muttering incoherent thanks in a faint voice, and Sir Robert became suddenly conscious that there was a fresh danger to be averted.

"Keep your head. Steady! Hold tight! You're all right," he cried as he still ran with the bicycle, upon which he was now acting as a brake.

But his words fell on ears that scarcely heard; and before he could bring the machine absolutely to a standstill, when he was within three or four yards of the traction-engine, which had been stopped, the rider fell to the ground with a moan.

There was a crowd round the group already, and there were shrieking women and curious men streaming towards the spot, where Sir Robert, with an air of authority, was giving directions to such of the more intelligent among the crowd as seemed likely to be of use in the emergency. Thus, he sent one man for a doctor and another for his own servants, while he himself knelt down by the roadside, and raised the unconscious victim of the accident.

She had struck her head against the kerb-stone, and one side of it was cut and bleeding.

"Poor child! She isn't dead. She'll be all right presently," said Sir Robert, answering the alarmed comments of the women who pressed round him. "I'm going to have her taken into my house, where the doctor will see her."

The accident had occurred within twenty yards of the entrance to Sir Robert's house, and five minutes later the baronet and his butler were carrying the unconscious girl under the little portico and up the staircase into a pleasant room at the back of the house, overlooking the grounds and the flowing stream.

A couple of children, a boy and a girl, the orphaned nephew and niece of Sir Robert and permanent members of his household, watched the arrival from the upper staircase with eager interest.

"Look at the blood, Minnie!" observed the boy, in an awestruck whisper. "And look at her eyes—all shut!" he added with thrilling interest.

The girl, younger and more tender-hearted, began to cry.

"She's dead!" sobbed she. "Oh, George, don't yook at her. She's been killded."

"No, she hasn't," said he sturdily. "Uncle Robert won't let her die."

Their hissing whispers had by this time attracted attention, and Bessie, the old family nurse in whose charge they were, beckoned to them from below with an austere frown.

"If you don't both go back into the nursery this minute——"

There was no need to say more: in an instant the scampering of small feet, followed by the banging of an upper door, showed that the young people, who were known in the household as The Terrors, were for the moment quelled.

In the meantime the victim of the accident had been laid upon a bed in a darkened room, and Bessie and her master were looking at her with sympathetic interest.

"Why, the poor dear's but a lass, sir," said the sympathetic Bessie, as she loosened the girl's clothes and peered keenly into the pale face.

"Yes, not more than eighteen or nineteen, I should think," said Sir Robert. "She had a narrow escape. Search her clothes, Bessie, for some indication as to her name and address. Her people will be alarmed about her, whoever she is, and whoever they may be."

"Yes, sir. I'll have a hunt as soon as the doctor's here."

She had not to wait long. And by the time the doctor had come, examined the patient, and reported that the victim was suffering from concussion of the brain and must be kept quiet, that she had sustained an injury to the right wrist and severe bruises, the old nurse had made a search of the girl's pockets, and had discovered an opened letter in one of them directed to "Miss Rhoda Pembury" at an address in Deal.

This was enough for Sir Robert, who telegraphed at once to the address, to the name of Pembury, to the effect that Miss Rhoda had met with a slight accident, but that she was safe and going on well.

Within a couple of hours the girl's father and mother had arrived at the Mill-house, and proved to be a London physician and his wife, who were staying at Deal with their family, of whom Rhoda was the eldest.

They were deeply grateful to Sir Robert, who insisted that they should leave their daughter where she was until she was fully recovered, a suggestion which poor Mrs. Pembury, the harassed mother of half a dozen children, gratefully accepted, it being arranged that Dr. Pembury should cycle over every day to see how his daughter was getting on.

Within a few days Rhoda, very pale still, and with deep dark lines under her large, plaintive, blue eyes, was sitting at the window of the room that had been assigned to her, permitted for the first time to leave her bed.

She was a tall, thin slip of a girl, not yet fully developed, but languid and almost sickly of appearance by reason of the rapidity of her recent growth. At seventeen she was five feet seven inches in height, with a lean, fair-skinned face, a mass of pale golden hair that looked as if a silver veil had been thrown over it, and a look of listlessness that told of weakly health.

She confessed to Bessie that she had only had her hair "up" within the last month, and that, in her present enfeebled condition, she preferred to leave it loose again, tied with a black ribbon, to the fatigue of doing it herself, or even of having it done for her.

So that she looked like a child as she sat at the open window, with her white dressing-gown on, and her head thrown back against the pillows provided for her.

In the garden below were two figures, upon whom her attention was fixed with interest so deep that Bessie watched her in furtive surprise, wondering at the look of vivid excitement which was making the blue eyes glow and the white skin flush.

The old nurse looked out, and saw that the objects of the girl's interest were Sir Robert Hadlow, sauntering in the grounds in his linen coat and broad-brimmed hat, and his handsome young ward, Jack Rotherfield, a tall, well-made man of two and twenty, whose dark-skinned, beardless face and curly black hair and dark eyes had earned him the reputation of the handsomest man in Kent.

The expression upon the girl's face, as she gazed out at the two men, was so unmistakably one of admiration of the most vivid kind, that Nurse Bessie smiled indulgently.

"A good-looking fellow, isn't he?" she said with a nod in the direction of the two figures.

To her surprise, the girl turned towards her with a look of ecstasy in her thin face.

"Good-looking!" she echoed in an awestruck tone. "Oh, don't call him that! He's so much more than that! It seems to me," she added, in a low voice, as again her eyes wandered in the direction of the two gentlemen, "that I've never seen, no, and never even imagined, any face either so handsome or—so—noble. It's because he's so good, so much better and greater than other men that he is so handsome."

The old nurse sat amazed and perplexed by this enthusiasm, which exceeded so far even her own warmth of admiration. She did not dare to smile, although the girl's tone was so outrageously, childishly vehement as to throw her into considerable astonishment.

"Well, Mr. Rotherfield is generally thought to be nice-looking," she said, "but I don't know as he's all you take him for."

The girl's fair face, out of which the glow of colour brought by her enthusiasm had already faded a little, looked at her with a frown of slight perplexity.

"Mr. Rotherfield? Who is that?" she asked.

Old Bessie stared.

"Why, the gentleman you've admired so much, the young gentleman that's walking with Sir Robert. That's his ward, Mr. Rotherfield."

A deeper flush than had yet appeared in Rhoda's face now spread quickly over it, and she lowered her eyelids quickly.

"I didn't notice him," she said. "I was speaking about Sir Robert."

The old nurse uttered a low cry of surprise.

Then a smile, indulgent, amused, appeared on her face.

"Well, it's the first time I've ever heard him called so nice-looking," she said. "He's very well, of course, and he's got a good face, and a nice face, but I've never heard tell he was considered handsome."

The girl looked up again, the most innocent surprise in every feature.

"Not handsome!" she said under her breath. "Why, it seems to me I never saw any face so—so beautiful! He's like a picture, not like any man I ever saw before. To look at him makes me feel humiliated at the thought that I should have been the means of causing him to hurt himself, and yet it makes me proud too to think that he should have done what he did for me!"

Beginning timidly, the girl grew more and more enthusiastic as she went on, till she ended with fire in her blue eyes, and sat with her lips parted in a sort of ecstasy, gazing out of the window at the figure of the wholly unconscious gentleman who was now sauntering back towards the house.

Sir Robert, who had hurt his arm in his efforts to stop the runaway bicycle, carried it in a sling, and Rhoda's eyes softened and filled with tears as she noted the fact.

5

The old nurse's face began to grow prim.

"You mustn't let Lady Sarah hear you speaking so admiring of her intended, or she'll be jealous," said she.

A sudden shadow passed over the girl's face.

"Lady Sarah! Who is she?" she asked quickly, in a stifled voice.

Bessie peered at her rather anxiously.

"Dear, dear, miss, you mustn't get so excited about it, or I shall feel I didn't ought to have told you so much," she said.

A faint, mechanical smile appeared on Rhoda's face.

"Nonsense," she said. "Of course I'm not excited, only interested. Who *is* Lady Sarah?"

The nurse hesitated a moment, but seeing that a red spot was beginning to burn in each of the invalid's cheeks, she decided that it would be better to tell her what she wanted and have done with it.

"Lady Sarah," she said, gravely and deliberately, hoping that the style and title of the persons she was about to mention would duly impress her hearer, "is the youngest daughter of the Marquis of Eridge, and she is engaged to be married to Sir Robert Hadlow, who is madly in love with her."

A look of dismay, so ingenuous, so complete as to be touching, appeared on Rhoda's face. Then she glanced quickly at the nurse, reddened deeply, and subduing her feelings, whatever those might be, answered in a matter-of-fact tone, in words which surprised Bessie.

"The Marquis of Eridge! Oh, yes, I know. He was made bankrupt two years ago, and he has four of the most beautiful daughters possible."

Bessie was taken aback by the completeness of the girl's information.

"I'm sure I don't know anything about the Marquis's affairs," she said, somewhat stiffly. "But a Marquis is a Marquis, and Lady Sarah is a most beautiful young lady. And Sir Robert is crazy about her, and to look at her it's no wonder. But you'll see her for yourself, I dare say, before you go away. She lives up in the Vale, at the Priory, and she and Lady Eridge are here most days when Sir Robert doesn't go to the Priory."

Rhoda bent her head without speaking. And the nurse, though she reproached herself for the feeling and said to herself that it was 'rubbish,' felt a momentary wonder whether it would not have been better for Sir Robert, with his studious habits and his grave demeanour, to have loved an earnest, simple little girl like the blue-eyed, fair-haired Rhoda with the devotion in her eyes, rather than the brilliant and slightly disturbing creature whom he had chosen for his wife.

CHAPTER II.
RHODA PEMBURY'S DISCOVERY

THE day after this conversation with Bessie, Rhoda was allowed downstairs for the first time. Sir Robert was kindness itself to her, though he was rather puzzled by the extreme reserve and timidity of the girl whose life he had saved, never guessing, in his masculine obtuseness, at the sentimental cause of her rather perplexing demeanour.

Jack Rotherfield, who was staying with his guardian, was delighted to welcome a new and pretty guest, and at once proceeded to exert himself to amuse and interest the convalescent, so that old Bessie used to smile demurely when she came into the room where the two young people would be sitting together, Rhoda gentle and rather listless, Jack energetically trying to rouse her from the somewhat abstracted state in which she still remained.

Rhoda laughed at the idea of falling in love with Jack, a possibility which Bessie plainly foresaw and made no scruple about mentioning.

"He's very nice," she said, "and, I suppose, very good-looking. But I don't like him as much as I ought to do, considering how kind he is. He always seems to me to be saying things to me which he must have said before."

Bessie looked surprised.

"Lor, miss, that's not a bad guess, I'm afraid, if it is a guess," she admitted. "Mr. Jack is so nice-looking, and so merry and bright, that the young ladies do make a fuss of him. Even Lady Sarah," she added in a rather lower tone.

A deep flush at once overspread Rhoda's face.

"I should hardly think," she said quite tartly, "that a girl who had the good fortune to be liked by Sir Robert would care much for Mr. Rotherfield."

Bessie looked askance at her, but said nothing more on the subject, until she presently remarked in a rather dry tone that Lady Sarah was coming that afternoon, with her mother and one of her married sisters, to play tennis and to have tea in the grounds.

Rhoda was excited by the news. She was exceedingly anxious to see the woman with whom Sir Robert was in love, and Bessie noted the trembling of her hands and the feverish light in her eyes as she dressed to go downstairs.

Lady Sarah Speldhurst proved to be a very fascinating and lovely little person. Not nearly so tall as Rhoda herself, nor with the advantage of so good a figure as the younger girl, she was, at three and twenty, mistress of all the arts by which a pretty young woman makes the best of herself.

Dark-eyed, with a brilliant complexion, and with masses of wavy dark brown hair, she dressed in light colours for choice, and was wearing, on this occasion, a tight-fitting lace dress of creamy tint over a slip of lemon colour, and a big black hat with black and white ostrich feathers.

"Sir Robert don't know what a lady's dress bill means—yet," remarked Bessie shrewdly, when she looked out and saw Lady Sarah in the garden.

"What an odd dress to play tennis in!" was Rhoda's matter-of-fact comment.

Bessie smiled.

"She don't play tennis much herself. Her ladyship likes the sitting about with a racquet in her hand, and the cakes and the ices, better than running in the sun and getting her face red," she said.

Rhoda frowned a little. Pretty as Lady Sarah was, the younger girl felt that a better, a more sincere and noble-natured person than Lady Sarah appeared to be would have been a better match for the generous and good Sir Robert who was her own idol. She went downstairs slowly, resented the quick and almost supercilious manner in which Lady Sarah appeared to sum her up at a glance while shaking hands, and decided angrily that Sir Robert was throwing himself away.

The baronet himself, however, was evidently by no means of the same way of thinking. There was adoration in his mild grey eyes as he watched the brilliant little brunette, there was tenderness in the tone of his voice as he spoke to her, and it was abundantly clear that his infatuation was complete.

Jack Rotherfield, meanwhile, was less attentive to Rhoda than he had been before the appearance of Lady Sarah. Rhoda did not mind this, but she remarked it, and, sitting silent for the most part, she noticed a good deal more, as the afternoon wore on, that might have escaped the notice of a less observant or more talkative person.

For one thing she saw, and felt ashamed of seeing, that something like a secret understanding existed between Jack Rotherfield and Lady Sarah; their eyes would meet with a sudden look of sympathy or mutual amusement from time to time, as, for instance, when Sir Robert declared that nothing would induce him to replace the old furniture and fittings of the house for more modern ones.

Rhoda felt ashamed of herself for thinking that it looked as if Lady Sarah had already discussed that very subject with Sir Robert's ward, and in a manner not very sympathetic with the views of her future husband.

Indeed it was clear to the most careless eyes that there was a great gulf between the tastes of the Marquis's lovely daughter, with her French toilette and her brilliant if scarcely sincere manners, and steady-going, quiet Sir Robert Hadlow with his grave demeanour and quiet habits.

Rhoda found herself wondering what sort of a household theirs would be, and which of the two would finally get the upper hand, as it was plain that, in such an ill-assorted couple, one or other must eventually do.

It seemed natural to suppose it would be the little, wilful, spoilt beauty, as it was easy to see she was not in love with Sir Robert, who, by keeping her head, would become the arbiter of the household destinies. The baronet seemed, indeed, to be like wax in her hands; and he was far too much in love to see that the sweet looks and pretty smiles, the little words of tenderness, and the gestures of caressing cajolery, were dictated by anything less than love equal to his own.

The rest of the party soon went into the grounds, and Rhoda, who was not yet allowed to exert herself much, was left alone in the house. She sat near the window, watching the pretty figures of the ladies in their light dresses as they flitted over the tennis-lawn, like gay butterflies against the background of soft greenery, when she heard a stealthy footstep behind her, and looking round, saw the Terrors, George and Minnie Mallory, crouching close to her chair.

"When did you come in?" asked Rhoda quickly. "I didn't hear you."

The two children chuckled.

"Nobody never does hear us," said Minnie, who was a long-legged, short-frocked imp of six years of age. "We don't never let 'em hear us," she added thoughtfully.

"But that's not right. It's like eavesdropping," said Rhoda solemnly.

George nodded gravely.

"It doesn't matter for us, 'cos we're only children," said he with a shrewd air. "And we often hear things that we like to hear. We heard Lady Sarah talking to Jack the other day, and saying how hard it was for her to have to marry a rich man, 'cos rich men are always what you don't like."

Rhoda uttered a sort of gasp. Then she recovered herself, and scolded the boy.

"It's very naughty to listen," she said. "And very ungentlemanly too. What would your uncle, who's always so good and kind to you, say if he thought his niece and nephew were not behaving like a lady and gentleman?"

George was not abashed.

"I'll behave like a gentleman when I grow up," he said reflectively. "I don't see the good of beginning too soon. It's nicer to do as we like and hear what we want to."

The comical gravity with which he spoke suddenly made Rhoda want to laugh, so she was silent for a moment, and the children took advantage of this to steal away out of the room, no doubt to follow their favourite dubious occupations elsewhere.

But Rhoda did not heed them. She was filled with a terrible thought. Her hero, the man she worshipped as the ideal of all that was noble and worthy, was being deceived, grossly deceived, by the woman he passionately loved. She had no doubt at all that the words reported by the mischievous boy had really been uttered by Lady Sarah, in confidential talk to Jack Rotherfield, between whom and herself it was plain that an active flirtation was still going on.

Her heart was torn by the thought that her hero, instead of being loved as he deserved to be loved, was being married for his money alone by the woman he worshipped. If only he could learn the truth before it was too late!

But how?

She could not tell him what she knew or guessed, and even if she could, he would not believe her.

What could she do?

Staying day by day under the same roof with Sir Robert, she had fallen more and more completely under the influence of his great kindness and gentleness, of the nature that was ever self-sacrificing, ever considerate for others, yet with a certain manliness and firmness that made Rhoda wonder what he would be like if he should ever find out that those he loved and trusted had deceived him.

She was still torn with her fears on his account when the baronet came in, racquet in hand, and sitting down beside her, asked her kindly how she felt.

The girl, pale and trembling, looked into his gentle, kindly face, and the words that came to her lips refused to come further.

He smiled at her, and patted her hand.

"You've been overtiring yourself. I shan't let you come downstairs to-morrow," he said.

Rhoda struggled to regain her self-command and answered steadily:

"I must come down to-morrow, Sir Robert, for I must go back home."

"You are tired of us? That you are in such a hurry to get away?"

She shook her head.

"You are the best and the kindest people I've ever met," she said tremulously. "But I want to go back."

He looked at her keenly.

"You have something on your mind," said he.

Rhoda rose suddenly to her feet. Looking down upon him with eyes that blazed, she said hoarsely:

"Yes. I want to warn you. Find out, Sir Robert, whether you are loved as you deserve to be loved. That's all."

The baronet rose, frowning and displeased. She saw that he looked upon her words as an impertinence, and she was cut to the heart.

Faltering, she stammered out an incoherent apology. Sir Robert looked at her coldly.

"There is nothing to apologise for," he said gravely. "I'm sure you mean well. I was taken by surprise, that's all."

Rhoda felt that the room was spinning round her. She knew his danger, and she saw that she was helpless to save him. There was only one thing to be done; she must go away. She could not stay another day now that she had offended him, nor could she watch the progress of the harm she could not prevent.

On the pretext of fatigue, she staggered upstairs, assisted by Sir Robert, as far as the foot of the staircase, where she gently refused further help.

Rhoda had never seen the kindly Sir Robert angry before, and the effect his displeasure had upon her was overwhelming. She, however, was not to be the only person to offend him that day, for Bessie, who came in with a little tray with the wing of a chicken for the convalescent, brought with her the news that Sir Robert was gravely displeased with his old servant, Langton, to whom he had given notice to leave him.

"I don't know the rights of it," went on Bessie, "and I don't want to gossip. But it's thought Langton told Sir Robert something he didn't want to hear, and didn't believe, and this is the consequences!"

Rhoda listened in distressed silence. Had the faithful servant dared to tell his master something that he had seen? Something that concerned Lady Sarah and Jack Rotherfield? She would not condescend to gossip with Bessie about it, but when she was alone, she left her repast almost untasted, and, attracted by a soft murmur of voices that came like a distant whisper through the open window, crossed the floor and looked out, and saw, between the branches of the trees, two figures sauntering along the avenue that ran inside the outer wall of the grounds.

She had no difficulty in recognising them, and when, before they had gone many steps, they stopped and the man put his arm round the girl and kissed her, Rhoda knew that it was Jack Rotherfield whom she had seen kissing the betrothed wife of his guardian.

Rhoda could bear no more; turning from the window, giddy and almost sick with grief and horror, she resolved to leave the house that very night. She felt that she could not meet the eyes of the baronet, his *fiancée*, or Jack Rotherfield again.

The evening seemed a long one; she had to go to bed, to avoid exciting suspicion as to her intention, which was to steal out of the house when everybody else was asleep. But before retiring she witnessed a sight that set her thinking. For after dinner Sir Robert walked with Lady Sarah up and down the terrace close under Rhoda's window, and the girl fancied, both by the affectionate manner in which they smiled at each other, and by the defiant half-glances which the baronet cast stealthily up towards her window, that he had told his *fiancée* of the doubts expressed as to her sincerity, and that Lady Sarah had set him quite at rest upon that score.

Rhoda did not sleep. At one o'clock, when all was silent in the house, she rose, dressed herself hastily, and glided softly out of her room and down the stairs. She had written a letter, directed to Sir Robert, and left it in her room. She had said in it that, having had the misfortune to offend him, she could not meet him again, but that she begged his pardon with all her heart, and hoped that he would forgive her, as she felt sure he would do, if he could only understand the pain she felt at having given a moment's displeasure to one to whom she owed so much. She added that she would never forget his goodness to her as long as she lived.

She had reached the hall, with the intention of leaving the house by the front-door, and had withdrawn the bolts, when she was startled by the sound of some one rapidly descending the stairs. She thought she was discovered, and hastily hid herself in the dark corner beside the tall grandfather's clock that stood near the door.

But she had scarcely done so when she caught sight of something which she could dimly discern to be a man, disappearing into the drawing-room, and the next moment she heard sounds within the room as of a scuffle and stifled cries.

Trembling and horror-struck, Rhoda was unable to decide whether she ought to go upstairs and call for help, when, panting and drawing deep breaths the figure stole out of the room again, shutting the door softly.

The man was in such deep darkness and Rhoda was so far entrenched in her corner that she could see but little of him, and that little very dimly, until he was half-way up the stairs, when, dragging his way up by the stair-rails, he laid his hand for a moment upon that spot of the banisters where a single ray of moonlight fell upon them from between the heavy velvet curtains that draped the staircase window.

And Rhoda saw, with a shudder, that across the hand was the red line of a cut which was still bleeding.

Before she could even be sure whether the figure was that of Sir Robert, as she believed, it had disappeared.

Confused, trembling, wondering what it was that had happened, Rhoda opened the front-door and slipped out, closing it softly behind her.

She thought that she must have made enough noise for the shutting of the door to have attracted attention, and she hoped, as she went slowly down the narrow slip of garden which was all that lay between the front of the house and the road, that the baronet would come out after her, waylay her, and perhaps insist upon her return.

But nobody came out, nobody followed her; and so, mystified, sick with terror, and asking herself as she went whether she ought to have come out without an effort to find out what had happened, she went down the road towards the harbour.

She put up, for the rest of the night, at an hotel where she had stayed before with her parents, and where travellers from off the boats came at all times of the night, so that her late arrival attracted no particular attention.

On the following morning she took the first train to Deal, and reached the lodgings where her parents were in such a condition of exhaustion that she was promptly put to bed. She insisted, however, upon being allowed to tell her mother the singular circumstances that had occurred at the moment of her departure from Mill-house, and begged that they would let her know at once if it should come to her parents' ears that anything serious had happened that night at Sir Robert's residence.

For four days she was kept in bed, and assured that nothing had happened as far as any one knew.

But when she was well enough to get up again, the truth was gradually broken to her. The dead body of the butler, Langton, had been found in the drawing-room, where it was evident that some sort of a scuffle had taken place. The drawing-room window had been found open, and it was supposed that a burglar had got in, and that the butler, hearing a noise, had gone down and had been murdered by the intruder.

The inquest had been held, and the verdict brought in: "Wilful murder by some person or persons unknown."

But the rumour about the neighbourhood was that there had been a serious quarrel between Langford and his master, that he was known to have been under notice to leave his situation, and that it was in a scuffle between master and man that Langford came by his death.

Rhoda sprang up with a cry.

"It's not true!" she cried. "Sir Robert is incapable of such a thing! Besides, I know! I can prove—Oh let me go and tell what I know!"

But the next moment the light faded out of her eyes and she sank back, trembling.

What did she know? What could she prove? Nothing, nothing.

CHAPTER III.

TEN YEARS AFTER

TEN years passed before Rhoda Pembury saw Sir Robert Hadlow or the old Mill-house again, and during those ten years all that she heard of him or of his doings was through an announcement in the newspapers, some six months after her stay there, of his marriage with Sarah, third daughter of the Marquis of Eridge.

After that, although Rhoda did, from time to time, see brief paragraphs in the papers concerning the doings of Lady Sarah Hadlow, and incidental mention in connection with her, of her husband, Sir Robert, she held no communication with them, or with any of the household at the Dourville Mill-house, and she believed, during the whole of that period, that the baronet who had saved her life and who had been kind to her, had passed out of her life for ever.

In the meantime, having developed into a beautiful and accomplished woman from the half-fledged girl she had been then, Rhoda received a good deal of attention and more than one offer of marriage.

But she cared little for admiration, and her heart was never touched. Greatly to the annoyance of her parents, who had a large family, and who were both eager to settle their handsome daughter in marriage and a home of her own, Rhoda made light of all the attentions paid to her, refused her lovers without compunction, and announced, when reproached with her coldness and obstinacy, that she intended to remain single through life, and that, as her parents would never be able to get her off their hands in the way they desired, she would meet their wishes by earning her own living.

This was not at all what they wanted, and her mother prevailed upon Rhoda to give way on this point for a time. But the thought was ever in the girl's mind, and Mrs. Pembury was not surprised when, ten years after the episode at the Mill-house, Rhoda came to her with a newspaper in her hand, and, pointing to an advertisement in one of the columns, said briefly:

"Mother, I'm going to answer this."

The announcement to which she pointed ran like this:

"A lady wanted, as nurse-companion to an invalid boy. Apply personally, if possible, at the Old Mill-house, Dourville."

Mrs. Pembury having put on her glasses, read the advertisement, and laid down the paper with an exclamation of something like dismay.

"Why, it's Sir Robert Hadlow's, where the murder was committed! Surely you wouldn't go back there!"

Rhoda, who was very pale, asked briefly:

"Why not?"

But Mrs. Pembury was too much disturbed to reply. Hastily leaving the room with some excuse, she went straight to her husband, who was in his surgery, and laid the paper before him.

"What do you think of that?" she asked in consternation. "I'd always had an idea it was something that happened while she was there that prevented Rhoda's marrying, and now I'm sure of it. I believe she fell in love with Sir Robert's ward, Mr. Rotherfield."

But Dr. Pembury thought this idea high-flown and far-fetched, and said he could not see any likelihood of such a thing. Rhoda would have betrayed herself before this if she had nourished a passion for so long, and in any case, it did not matter, as it was more than likely that Sir Robert had left the Mill-house by this time, since his wife appeared to be always in London, or, if not, that Mr. Rotherfield had settled down somewhere else with a wife of his own.

Mrs. Pembury was troubled, but she always submitted, even against her better judgment, to her husband's wishes, and in this case it was not even her judgment, but only a sort of feminine instinct, which told her that Rhoda had strong sentimental reasons for wishing to take this step.

On the following day, therefore, Rhoda, who was now twenty-seven, and better capable of looking after herself than she had been at seventeen, started alone for Dourville, and presented herself, early in the afternoon, at the house she remembered so well.

Emotion made her eyes fill and her limbs tremble as she approached the house, and recognised that it had undergone such changes, since she first knew it, that she could scarcely be sure she had not made a mistake and come to the wrong gate, when she found herself standing before a long, white house, with wings extending far in each direction, and with the modern big, wide windows replacing the little narrow old ones.

Many of the trees that had surrounded the old house so closely had been cut down, with considerable advantage as regards light, but at a great loss of picturesqueness. Gone was the cosy, old-fashioned look, together with the dark red curtains, the heavy square portico, the homely look that she had loved.

It was into a stately, handsome hall that she was shown, a room having been sacrificed to enlarge the entrance; and when she found herself following a footman across a wide expanse of parquetted floor to a new part of the building, and ushered into a lofty, light library, Rhoda was almost ready to believe that she had made a mistake, and that the Sir

Robert, who would, so the footman said, see her at once, could not be the man who had saved her life, the memory of whose kindness she had treasured in secret for so long, the man whose image had, almost unknown to herself, so effectually shut out that of every other man from her heart during these ten years.

But there he was, not indeed the Sir Robert she remembered, but perfectly recognisable to her, although the dark hair had become thickly streaked with grey, and the face more deeply lined than that of a man of forty-five ought to be.

She had felt her heart beating very fast as she was led towards the library, but she was totally unprepared for the reception she met.

She was duly announced as "Miss Pembury," but she perceived at once that the name awoke no memories in Sir Robert.

He had forgotten her.

In part, perhaps, the fact that he was very short-sighted, and that he was not wearing his glasses, was answerable for his lack of recognition, but however that might be, Rhoda felt cut to the heart when he rose, bowed formally, and offered her a chair.

"I am sorry that my wife is away, as she would have been better capable than I of arranging these matters with you, Miss Pembury," he said. "Ladies can get to the point over such things more quickly than a mere man can hope to do. But I'll tell you all I can, and you will perhaps be able to judge whether you would care to come to take charge of my boy. But perhaps you would like to see him first? He is an invalid, as I suppose you know."

"I should like to see him," said Rhoda, in a low and gentle voice.

But the voice recalled no memories, and Sir Robert, ringing the bell, told the servant to have Master Caryl's carriage brought along the terrace.

Rhoda was still so much under the influence of the strong emotions called up by this meeting that she was glad there was no need for her to say much.

On learning that she lived in London, and that she had come all the way from the great city that morning, Sir Robert seemed surprised, and ringing the bell again, told the footman to have some luncheon prepared for Miss Pembury.

Rhoda protested, and thanked the baronet, who seemed already to take it for granted that she would stay. The fact being that her refined manner, sweet voice and sympathetic appearance had at once predisposed the rather absent-minded gentleman in the visitor's favour.

A few minutes later there was a slight sound of footsteps upon the terrace, and Rhoda, looking out, saw, with tears in her eyes, a boy lying on a long, spinal chair, looking in at her through the window with big, soft, dark eyes that, while they recalled in colour and brilliancy those of his mother, had something of the far-away expression of his father in them too.

She hastened across the floor, and bending over the boy kissed him on the forehead.

He flushed a little, put out his hand and laid it upon hers.

"Are you coming to stay with me?" he asked simply.

"It is for you to say, dear," said Rhoda.

He moved his head slowly and looked at her with great intentness.

"I should like it very much," he said. "What am I to call you?"

Rhoda threw a hasty glance at Sir Robert, who was standing by them, so intent in watching his son's face that he took but little heed of the visitor. So she thought she might venture to give her name without fear of discovery. Since he had begun by non-recognition, it was better to go on without undeceiving him, she thought.

"Call me Rhoda," she said softly.

He smiled at her. Though he was scarcely more than eight years old, his condition had made him older in many ways than his age, and his manner was almost that of a grown person as he said:

"Rhoda. Yes, I like that."

"You will stay with him then?" asked Sir Robert, evidently pleased at the fancy the child had taken to the lady.

Rhoda hesitated. There were details to be settled, of which the man took no cognizance. Perceiving her hesitation, he smiled, and waving his hand, said:

"You will want to know a great many things, about hours and holidays and—and other things. We can leave all those until Lady Sarah comes back next week, can't we? My housekeeper will assign you rooms, any you care for, and you can do just as you please, as long as you make my boy happy. He is left too much alone. His mother doesn't like Dourville; it doesn't agree with her very well. I hope it will please you, however."

"Thank you. I shall like it, I know," said Rhoda.

"Come and talk to me," said Caryl, "and let me show you my monkey, and my rabbits. I've got three, and some budgerigars. I hope you like birds. And I've got a dog. Would you like to see him? I want you to see him do his tricks."

Off they went together, the lady and the child, and Sir Robert, standing blinking in the sunshine, seemed to have, Rhoda thought, a vague impression of having seen or heard something which the lady's presence recalled.

But to her regret, it was evident that the recollection was fraught with pain.

She and the boy made the tour of the garden together, for he had dismissed the servant, asking Rhoda if she would draw him along.

By the time they had been an hour together, moving slowly along the shady walks, and visiting the boy's numerous pets in rabbit-hutch and aviary, they were already firm friends; and when they returned to the terrace, Rhoda had the satisfaction of seeing Sir Robert standing at the library window, with a faint smile upon his face. He was pleased by the pleasure of his boy.

"It's good of you to humour him by walking about so long when you must be tired, Miss Pembury," he said. "I have sent for Mrs. Hawkes, the housekeeper, and directed her to have some tea for you, and to show you your rooms."

"Thank you very much," said Rhoda.

She had a transient fancy that Sir Robert recalled something in her name or in her person, for he looked at her suddenly with a slight frown and with vague curiosity. He did not, however, ask her any questions, and a few minutes later Rhoda was going upstairs, escorted by the footman, towards the rooms where the housekeeper was busy preparing for her reception.

The man threw open a door and announced:

"Miss Pembury, Mrs. Hawkes," and Rhoda entered.

The man went away, and Rhoda heard an exclamation from the grey-haired woman in spectacles who was drawing a cover over a little table in the pretty sitting-room.

"Why, it's Miss Rhoda!" cried the grey-haired woman.

The visitor exclaimed in her turn.

"Bessie!" cried she.

Neither woman could restrain her tears.

"I'm housekeeper here now," said Bessie, wiping her eyes. "But, oh, Miss Pembury, to think Sir Robert shouldn't know you! And to think of your turning up here, after all this time, and us wanting you so bad ten years ago!"

"What do you mean?" asked Rhoda, trembling.

"Let me get your rooms ready, and get rid of the maid, who is in the next room and who will be in here in a minute, and then I'll tell you everything," said Mrs. Hawkes.

And within five minutes, the two rooms having been got ready, and the maid dismissed in search of tea and sandwiches for Miss Pembury, the two old friends sat down in the window-seat together, and the housekeeper began her story.

CHAPTER IV.
RHODA RETURNS TO MILL-HOUSE

"AH, Miss Pembury, there's been a many changes since the night when you ran away from here!" she said, as she sighed and folded her hands in her lap. "But why did you go so quick and so quiet? And why didn't you come forward when the inquest was held?"

"I—I went away because I'd displeased Sir Robert," said Rhoda. "So that I couldn't bear to meet him again. And as for the inquest, if you mean that on the poor butler, I never heard anything about it till long after it was over. I fell ill, you know, and they wouldn't let me know anything."

Mrs. Hawkes nodded.

"I know that was what they said, but we all thought that it was only an excuse, and that the truth was you didn't want to come forward, because you knew too much."

"Too much!" faltered Rhoda.

"Yes. By the time you were missed, and by what we heard of your arriving at the hotel where you stayed the night, we thought as how you couldn't but have heard or seen something of the murderer of poor Langton."

Rhoda trembled at the recollection.

"Who was the murderer?" she asked in a whisper.

The housekeeper shook her head.

"Nobody knows from that day to this," she answered. "The inquest was held, after being put off, and they brought it in 'by some person unknown.' But people talked, and it was very unpleasant for us all."

"What did they say?" asked Rhoda hoarsely.

The housekeeper closed the window, and went to the door, looked out and came back again.

"These aren't things one likes to talk about, even now," she said. "Of course the thing was really clear enough. It was a thief tried to rob the house, did get in a little way, and poor Langford went down and struggled with him and got killed."

"How was he killed?" asked Rhoda.

"He must have been flung down into the fireplace with so much force that it killed him, they said. He was found with his head in the stone fireplace, covered with blood and dead. Fractured skull, the doctors said he died of. But his hands were gashed as if he'd been struggling with some one for a knife."

Rhoda was listening, in a state of stupefaction with horror. But she would not betray herself. Sitting very still, with her head bent, she listened.

The housekeeper went on:

"No knife was found, and though they saw some footsteps coming to the house, they found none going away again. That was odd and mysterious. Especially," the housekeeper looked round her again, and dropped her voice, "as Sir Robert had been out in the grounds very late."

"Sir Robert!" echoed Rhoda, appalled.

Mrs. Hawkes nodded.

"That was the part of it that made us all uncomfortable," she said, below her breath. "And that was why they wanted you to come forward. And you would have had to come, only your father said you knew nothing about it at all, and that it would have endangered your life to have had to come."

"Oh!" gasped Rhoda.

"For everybody thought even more than they said. Everybody wanted to know if you had seen anybody."

She paused, and tried to look into Rhoda's face. But the girl kept her head obstinately bent. Not for the world would she have had the nurse see the look of horror which she felt there must be in her own eyes.

It was not that she thought that Sir Robert had killed his servant: not for one moment would she have admitted such a possibility. But she could herself have borne witness to the fact that some one did go upstairs after the struggle in the drawing room.

Who could it have been?

"There was lots of talk and idle gossip," went on Mrs. Hawkes. "And even after the verdict was given, the talk went on just the same. You see it was known that nobody had any quarrel with Langford except the master, and it was known that Langford had had his notice, though why he got it was not rightly known."

There was a pause, but still Rhoda refrained from asking any questions.

"And it never has been known," added the housekeeper solemnly, "from that day to this."

"I couldn't have said anything to help," said Rhoda at last in a stifled voice.

"Didn't you see anything, or hear anything then?"

"Yes. I heard a noise in the drawing-room," admitted Rhoda, "and I went out by the front door."

"Yes, we knew that, for some one heard it shut. And that was one reason why we thought you must have known something."

Rhoda suddenly sat up.

"Surely," she said sharply, "nobody was so foolish and wicked as to think that Sir Robert, the best man in the world, had anything to do with it?"

The housekeeper answered quickly:—

"Of course we, who knew him, didn't think so. But there were plenty of unkind things said outside, you may be sure, miss."

"How shocking!"

"And folks thought as the marriage would be broken off, for the Marquis was a good deal cut up about the gossip. But then Lady Sarah she stood up like a high-minded lady, and she said as how she didn't allow such foolishness to disturb her for one moment. And she married him, and even married him the sooner for the talk. Which was handsome of her, and which Sir Robert he thought the world of in her, you may be sure."

Rhoda nodded. From what she had seen of the flippant and vivacious flirt she wondered whether high-mindedness was really the quality to which Sir Robert owed her steadfastness.

There was a pause, and Mrs. Hawkes gave a deep sigh, which made Rhoda look at her, and perceive that an expression of the deepest disappointment was on the good woman's features.

"I was in hopes as you would be able to tell something, something that would have cleared things up, miss," she said.

Rhoda's eyes filled with tears, while a hot blush rose to her cheeks. It was quite true that she did know something, just a little more than anybody else appeared to know, about the doings of that fatal night. But as it was nothing definite enough to absolve anybody or to convict anybody, she felt that wisdom lay in keeping that little to herself, for the present, at any rate.

"And so Lady Sarah was staunch, and earned Sir Robert's gratitude?" she said, her constraint making her words sound rather stiff.

Mrs. Hawkes looked enigmatic for a moment, and then came a little closer.

"Seeing you know so much about them, I may tell you, in confidence, that it's not been as happy a marriage as, from such a beginning, one might have hoped," she said. "You see it was a disappointment there being only the one child, this poor boy that never was strong. And then, well, Lady Sarah's tastes and Sir Robert's they don't seem to go well together. So my lady's most often away, either in town or abroad for her health, and Sir Robert, he don't seem to care to leave his house and his boy that he loves so much."

"And doesn't Lady Sarah care for her boy too?"

The housekeeper's face altered a little in expression.

"Of course she does," she replied diplomatically. "But there's different ways of caring, and the sight of him with his little couch and his spinal chair, well, it hurts my lady, who would have liked to have a boy handsome and tall and strong."

Rhoda felt chilled.

"It's a pity she ever married Sir Robert," she cried impulsively.

The housekeeper looked rather shocked.

"Well, miss, he wouldn't let her be till she'd promised him, he was so much in love," she said quickly. "And anyhow, he's pleased his fancy. He married the lady he liked best."

"Yes."

Another question was on Rhoda's tongue, but it was one she was shy of uttering.

It took a different form from the one at first in her mind when at last she said, timidly:

"Is Mr. Rotherfield married?"

Mrs. Hawkes looked at her quickly.

"No, he's not married," she said slowly. "I think he's in love too often to fix upon any one lady."

There was something in her face that prevented Rhoda from asking any more questions on that subject. Indeed, Mrs. Hawkes was not prepared to answer any more, for she changed the subject and said: "Do you remember the two children who were here at the time of your accident, miss?"

"Why, yes, of course I do. George and Minnie. What has become of them? The Terrors you used to call them."

"And the Terrors they are still," said Mrs. Hawkes emphatically. "They're away now; Master George he's at Sandhurst, and Miss Minnie she's staying in Normandy with friends for the summer holidays. But they live here still, and I don't say I'd be without them, though their battles with my lady don't give one much peace."

"Battles?"

"Yes, they're just what they always were, and the plague of all our lives."

"I wonder whether they'll recognise me!" said Rhoda.

"Trust them for it!"

"But Sir Robert doesn't."

Mrs. Hawkes looked at her.

"Well, there's no need to be astonished, for he's so short-sighted, and he lives so much shut up with his books and his collections, that he hasn't much memory for anything else. He's taken to collecting since you were here, miss, and he's got a gallery of pictures that people come for miles to see. That's what the north wing was built for, to put them in. And the south wing, that was for my lady's dances. Not that she gives many of them now."

There was a little constraint on both sides now that Rhoda had confessed that Sir Robert had failed to recognise her. Mrs. Hawkes looked disturbed. At last she said:

"I was wondering, if I may make so bold as say so, miss, whether Sir Robert would let you stay here again, if he was to remember you."

Rhoda looked startled and uneasy.

"Why should he mind?" she asked quickly.

"Oh, only that he doesn't in general like to be reminded of that time. And if he had recognised you, he couldn't but have thought of it, could he?"

"N-no," said Rhoda, beginning to feel nervous.

There was another silence, and then Mrs. Hawkes ventured:

"Would it be taking too great a liberty, miss, to ask how you came to want to come back here, after all these years? For you must have remembered too, what happened, and have felt uncomfortable about it, I should think?"

Rhoda blushed hotly.

"Of course I knew what happened, through the newspapers and what I was told," she said. "But I didn't think it could matter. How should it? I didn't know anything."

"No, miss."

Mrs. Hawkes looked down again.

"May I venture to ask whether you found the master altered, miss?"

Rhoda's lips trembled a little as she replied:

"Yes, I did. He doesn't look so young, of course, as he did then."

"Nor so happy," suggested the housekeeper almost under her breath. "And do you still think him as handsome as you did?"

Rhoda tried to laugh.

"You want to know, I suppose, whether I still feel the infatuation I felt then about him?" she said. "Of course I don't. It was a young girl's childish fancy. But I do think he is a most sympathetic, kindly natured man, and I should be very glad, considering what my obligations are to him, if I could be of any use in taking care of his child."

She was wondering, as she spoke, what Lady Sarah would say when she found her installed at the Mill-house. Until that moment, strange to tell, she had felt no curiosity on this point; it was only now, when she saw the view the housekeeper took of her coming, that this question suggested itself to her. However, there were some days to pass before Lady Sarah would return from abroad, and in the meantime Rhoda might pass her time very happily with the child, she thought.

And so it fell out. Within a few minutes her *tête-à-tête* with the housekeeper was interrupted by a message to the effect that Master Caryl wanted to see her, wanted to know whether she would have tea with him, and Rhoda, hastily divesting herself of her hat, went downstairs to the boy's room, where she found him, flushed and eager, awaiting her coming and welcoming her with a cry of delight.

The next few days were among the happiest she had ever passed. Caryl was a charming companion, affectionate, docile on the whole, though somewhat spoilt. He had taken a great fancy to Rhoda, and would not leave her much time to herself, while Sir Robert, delighted at his son's finding an interest in life, overwhelmed her with signs of his appreciation.

Rhoda wondered sometimes whether he did not begin to remember her; for she would find him regarding her as it were by stealth, with a frown of pain upon his face, and although he asked no questions, she felt sure that he must already be wondering whether he had not met her before.

To Rhoda the sadness in his quiet face was infinitely touching, and little by little she found ways of making herself useful to him, by copying the notes he had made concerning his curios, as well as by letting him talk to her concerning them.

"It's very good of you to let yourself be bored, Miss Pembury," he would say to her with a shy laugh when he had been expatiating upon the beauties of his enamels or of his old Sèvres china. "When Lady Sarah comes back, she will say that you have spoilt me. I'm not used to having my dull dissertations listened to with so much appearance of interest. And I'm quite sure," he added archly, "that it can't be more than an appearance."

"Indeed I wouldn't pretend to be interested if I were not, Sir Robert," Rhoda assured him humbly and earnestly.

And she told the truth. She would not, indeed, have found the pictures and curios so intensely interesting as she did, if they had not belonged to the man who had once saved her life. But for his sake she liked them, and her sympathy delighted the grave and rather lonely gentleman.

He was profusely grateful to her for the pains she took in collecting and copying his notes, and in sorting his papers for him. And he said to her with intense appreciation, one day when she had succeeded in deciphering some of his notes which he himself could not read:

"Miss Pembury, if you hadn't come here as companion to my boy, I should have had to keep you here as my secretary."

He could not guess the pleasure the simple words gave to the sensitive and grateful Rhoda. She had to pause a moment before she could reply with calmness:

"I wonder you have never before thought of having a secretary, Sir Robert."

He shook his head.

"I wouldn't have one for worlds," he answered with decision, "unless I could get one to undertake the duties of free will. What! To have a professional secretary fingering my papers, and handling my treasures coldly, because it was his or her duty to do it!" And with a little playful assumption of horror, he added: "Do you know, I really think it would injure the pictures and the china too, to be subjected to the perfunctory care of some one specially engaged to look after them? No. I'm fanciful about my treasures. Whatever work is done in connection with them, must be done for love."

The ingenuous words struck a responsive chord within the breast of Rhoda, and she did not say a word.

But the implied compliment to her thoughtful help was treasured up in her heart, and it made her happy for the day.

Lady Sarah's return was delayed for a week, so that, when at last Mrs. Hawkes received word that she was to prepare her rooms, Rhoda had been a fortnight at the Mill-house, and was already feeling quite at home.

She spent the day between Caryl and Sir Robert; very often now, indeed, Caryl would insist upon her taking him into his father's study, where he would lie in a corner watching Rhoda while she deciphered notes and copied inscriptions.

Sir Robert began to entrust more and more of his work to her, always prefacing any request with a humble apology for taking up so much of her time, and always receiving the quiet assurance that what he asked her to do was just what she had been wishing herself that she might do.

Caryl, his father said, was happier than he had ever been before.

"You fill just that place to him," said Sir Robert enthusiastically, one evening, "that I had always hoped would be filled by my niece Minnie. But of course you don't know her, so you don't understand."

Rhoda remained silent. She did know Minnie, and she knew, too, how hopeless it would have been to expect quiet sympathy from that young lady, if she had fulfilled her childish promise and grown up the mischievous torment she seemed to be inclined to develop into.

It seemed almost tragic to Rhoda that, while speaking thus of his niece, he left out all mention of his wife, who would have seemed to be the boy's natural companion.

"You'll be very, very glad to see mama again, won't you, Caryl?" Rhoda asked that evening, when he had been put to bed and she was bending over him to bid him good-night.

"It doesn't make so much difference to me whether she's here or not," replied the child, in the quaint, old-fashioned way children have who see few playfellows or companions of their own age.

Perhaps Rhoda looked rather shocked. So the boy added:

"Mama is not like you. She likes to be out in her motor-car all day, or playing tennis or dancing. She isn't quiet, like you."

"She will have brought you something pretty, I expect," suggested Rhoda.

"Oh, yes, but she never brings the things that I like," complained Caryl. "What I want is a book full of pictures of hunting. I know she won't bring me that."

Rhoda was struck with the pathos of this wish. For poor little Caryl, condemned to lie on his back and unable to run about and play like other children, had a passion for sport of all kinds, and was never happier than when watching a cricket or a football match; and even now, in early September, he was talking eagerly about the fox-hunting season, and asking Rhoda if she would take him to a meet of foxhounds when cub-hunting began.

She had begun by this time to dread Lady Sarah's return, to wonder whether her presence at the Mill-house would be resented by the flighty beauty, who would certainly remember her, and who might perhaps look upon her as an interloper, and be jealous of the help she gave to Sir Robert and of the love which little Caryl had already bestowed upon her.

It was the next day that the mistress of the house was to arrive and Rhoda was now on thorns. In the old days, indeed, Lady Sarah had scarcely spoken to her, but she might not look upon her with the same indifference now.

For Rhoda was conscious that there were whispers abroad concerning herself; and she guessed that, although the whole of the household, with the single exception of Mrs. Hawkes, was changed since she was there last, the housekeeper must have told some of the servants about the bicycle accident and the flight of Miss Pembury on the night of the tragedy at the Mill-house, and that there was a certain curiosity abroad concerning her.

It was late in the day when Lady Sarah arrived, and coming up to the bedroom of her little son when he had retired for the night, found Rhoda in the room.

Rhoda, however, regretting that she should have been found there, and fearing that Lady Sarah would think she was trying to take the mother's place already with the boy, kept in the background, and witnessed, unremarked by Lady Sarah, the meeting between mother and son.

"Well, Caryl, and how are you?" cried she, as she bent over him and gave him a light kiss on the forehead. "They tell me you've been getting on famously and that you've got an awfully nice companion now."

"Yes. I love Rhoda, and so will you, mama. Rhoda, come here. You shall see her, mama," cried the boy in excitement.

Lady Sarah stood up and Rhoda had a good view of her. She saw that the ten years which had passed since she met her first had only served to ripen her beauty. Lady Sarah, though not quite so slim and slender, so like a fairy as she had been in the days of her girlhood, was lovelier than ever. Her dark eyes were just as bright, her complexion was as brilliant, while a little dignity of manner now added to her charms.

She held out her hand graciously, and Rhoda came forward.

But the moment she came within the range of light thrown by the shaded electric lamp on the table at the foot of the bed, Lady Sarah's face changed. A look of intense horror appeared in her face, and her hand dropped, as she met Rhoda's eyes with a startled look, and, recognising her at once, said hoarsely, under her breath:

"Miss Pembury!"

CHAPTER V.

LADY SARAH'S RECOGNITION

RHODA was abashed and shocked by the expression on Lady Sarah's face. She had, indeed, felt rather nervous about the meeting, but she had not expected that the sight of her would cause so much dismay to Sir Robert's wife.

There was not the least doubt that she recognised the girl in a moment.

She forgot all about her child in her excitement at the meeting, and it was not until Caryl had plucked at her sleeve three or four times, that she bent over him again, and answered him.

"Yes, yes, dear. I know it is Rhoda," she said.

She had recovered herself, and the next moment she had come round the little bed, seized Rhoda's hand, and was shaking it with warmth as unexpected as her manifest horror had been.

"Miss Pembury! Why, of course, I might have remembered the name! But for the moment I didn't. It's the Miss Rhoda Pembury who fell off her bicycle and was brought in here by Sir Robert, years and years ago, before we were married, isn't it?"

"Ye-es," stammered Rhoda, quite bewildered by this rapid change in the lady.

"Why didn't he tell me? I should have been so much interested. He never said a word in his letters to let me know the pleasure in store for me."

This expression was rather a strong one, Rhoda thought, considering that on the solitary occasion of her seeing Lady Sarah at the Mill-house that lady had hardly condescended to address a single word to her.

She hastened to give the reason for Sir Robert's strange behaviour.

"He hasn't recognised me, Lady Sarah," she said.

"What!"

Lady Sarah paused a moment, in apparent incredulity, mingled with evident embarrassment and misgiving. Then she asked, quickly:

"Why didn't you remind him?"

"Well, I—I thought I'd wait till you came, to see whether you would remember me," she stammered.

"Of course I do. Although you have altered a great deal," said Lady Sarah, with a gracious smile. "You were rather a pretty girl then, but you didn't promise to develop as you have done."

Rhoda smiled and blushed. Nothing, certainly, could be more engaging than Lady Sarah's manner, nothing more flattering than her words. But still Rhoda could not but feel all the while that there was some reason for this surprising and even uncalled for graciousness. From all she had heard,

Sir Robert's wife, though a very charming and beautiful woman, was far from being always sympathetic or amiable in her own house, and there seemed to be no particular reason why she should be so very nice.

Rhoda, while rather ashamed of her misgivings, felt them quite strongly.

"I suppose you scarcely recognised the old place?" went on Lady Sarah, still in the same tone of smiling good humour, quite forgetting the small boy in his bed, who was lying with his eyes fixed upon Rhoda, waiting for the ladies to come back to him.

"It is very much changed," said the girl.

Lady Sarah laughed.

"Inside and out I've effected marvellous transformations, I flatter myself. You know my family has suffered horribly from want of money, as all decent families do now-a-days. If this horrid Budget with its Land clauses passes, why, Papa and Mama will simply have to pack a small handbag with necessaries, such as hair-dye and face powder, and trudge off to the nearest workhouse."

Rhoda laughed. But Lady Sarah affected to be shocked at her levity.

"Oh, it's quite true, indeed," she said. "However, that will explain to you how I felt when I got married and found myself at last with an occasional eighteenpence of my own. I went mad, mad, I really did. I made up my mind to have a house I could live in comfortably, and I was generous enough to let my husband have something he liked too. Do you know, before he married me, fond as he was of his pictures and china and things, it had never occurred to him to build a place to put them in? But I changed all that. I practically rebuilt the house, as you see; let in a little light and air into the musty corners; let him have a gallery which has become the joy of his heart. And—well, I didn't forget myself either, while I was about it."

And she laughed the merry, careless laugh of a happy child. It was all put on, but so well that Rhoda was fascinated, sure as she could not but feel that there was some reason for this lavish expenditure of Lady Sarah's fascinations upon a person so obscure as herself.

"Mama!" piped the small voice from the bed.

"Oh! Caryl! I'd forgotten him."

Lady Sarah took Rhoda by the hand, and brought her to the bed, and they both kissed the boy before they left him. He was as much surprised, Rhoda could not but feel, as she herself was, at the warmth of his mother's manner to the newcomer in the household.

Lady Sarah turned with a most graceful movement to the girl as they went out of the room.

"Nothing could have pleased me better," said she quite earnestly, "than to find he has some one with him to whom he can take a fancy. It's half the battle, with a poor child like Caryl, to have faces about him that he likes."

"It's very kind of you to say so."

"I suppose they didn't show you my rooms?" she went on. "Really you must see them. Come with me."

"Oh, some other time, Lady Sarah. You must be dreadfully tired after your journey!"

"Tired! Not a bit. I'm never tired. Come. I insist."

She carried Rhoda off to her own suite of apartments; and the girl was charmed, as indeed she was prepared to be, with the sumptuous elegance and refinement of taste, which were everywhere apparent in the furniture and fittings of the beautiful suite of rooms on the first floor which were specially consecrated to the use of the mistress of the house.

All was as different as possible from the richness and heaviness which were the prevailing notes downstairs. Lady Sarah explained this by saying that she had studied her husband's taste in the fitting up of the library, study and dining-room, as those were the only rooms in which he took an interest.

"I didn't like to part with all the old things. It would have broken his heart, for one thing; and for another, the old furniture, though of course it's just not old enough, is not so bad after all, and its mature years give a sort of dignity even to mahogany. But up here I am queen, and I have everything just as I like it. Come and see these sweet little French water-colours. Aren't they too divy for words?"

She turned on the electric light with her own hands, and let a flood of soft light upon the silk-panelled walls, pale blue and pink set in white enamel; upon the exquisite mantelpiece with its picture above in the manner of Fragonard; the dainty Sèvres clocks, all telling a different time; the cushions, couches, boudoir piano in a painted case, and all the other luxurious trifles that make up so much of the happiness of women of Lady Sarah's type.

Suddenly the dainty mistress of the place threw herself upon a couch, and beckoned with pretty imperiousness to Rhoda to sit beside her.

"Come here," she said. "I want to ask you something."

She had not yet divested herself of her hat and scarf, though she had thrown off her travelling cloak and given it to her maid as soon as she entered the house, even before receiving the welcoming kiss of Sir Robert.

Now she began to pull off her gloves, and as Rhoda slowly obeyed the invitation and sat down beside her, Lady Sarah suddenly bent her head, and said with infantile prettiness:

"Do help me to find the hatpins. I've been wearing this terrible hat all day!"

The little task was performed without the least difficulty, as the hatpins in question were huge discs of tortoiseshell and gold impossible to overlook. Then Lady Sarah, thanking her profusely, put the hat beside her on the couch, and ruffling up her dark hair with a sigh of relief, put one little white hand sparkling with diamonds through Rhoda's arm, and said coaxingly:

"And now do tell me what made you think of coming to us?"

"Oh-ho!" thought Rhoda. "This, then, is the reason of my amiable reception! You are curious."

But all she said was:

"I was happy here, ten years ago, and Sir Robert saved my life. I thought I should like to see the old house again, and when I got here, and saw your dear little boy, I was delighted to stay."

Lady Sarah was watching her with a piercing expression.

"Then when you came here you didn't know whether you would stay or not?"

"No. I didn't know anything. I didn't even know whether the house was still inhabited by Sir Robert. There was no name given in the advertisement."

It was quite clear to Rhoda that Lady Sarah did not believe her, but as her incredulity was not expressed in words, it was impossible to meet and combat it. They were both silent for a few moments while Lady Sarah smoothed out her gloves with a reflective air.

Suddenly Rhoda turned to her:

"Do you mind my coming? I wanted to know that."

"Mind! I'm quite delighted to have you here. The great anxiety I had about my boy was to get some one to be with him whom he could love, and I could trust. Well, who could fill the post better than you? I am delighted. And to find that you have been helping Sir Robert. He tells me you copy his notes for him. It's really too good of you, when he writes such a shocking hand too! I shall have to take you away with me when I go to town, on purpose to decipher his letters to me. I never get much farther myself than the bottom of the first page."

This was all she would say, and when Rhoda left her to dress for dinner, which had been put off till her return, the girl felt perplexed and uneasy.

For, while nothing could be more charming than her words and her manner, Rhoda felt it was not possible that so much enthusiasm could be quite genuine.

She would have felt still more puzzled if she could have overheard the conversation which took place immediately afterwards between Sir

Robert and his wife. Lady Sarah went into her dressing-room, and, being able to dress in the most surprisingly rapid fashion when she chose, emerged thence a quarter of an hour later radiant and refreshed, in a clinging gown of golden-brown satin, veiled in net of gold thread, and trimmed with a huge bunch of red velvet flowers on the left hand side of her bodice. With a butterfly of gold thread in her dark hair, and a single row of big diamonds round her throat, Lady Sarah looked as beautiful as a Princess in a fairy tale.

She glided quickly down the stairs before the dinner-gong sounded, and presented herself in the study in a sort of whirlwind.

"Robert," she said, "I have seen this lady whom you've engaged as companion to Caryl. Do you know who she is?"

The baronet was taken aback. His wife's manner was much more earnest than usual; and he, accustomed to her little flippant ways and to her manner of making light of everything, could not understand the change in her.

"Who she is!" he repeated in a dazed way. "She's a Miss Rhoda Pembury, and a most amiable and obliging young lady."

Lady Sarah stamped her pretty foot impatiently.

"Yes, yes, of course I know that. It's her *métier* to be obliging. But do you know who she is, and that she has introduced herself into the household on false pretences?"

Sir Robert looked amazed and incredulous.

"What false pretences?" stammered he at last.

She laid her hand impressively on his arm.

"Have you forgotten the girl who fell off her bicycle, the girl you saved from being run over?"

An exclamation, which was one almost of relief, broke from the baronet's lips.

"Of course," cried he. "Pembury, Miss Pembury! I knew I'd heard the name, I was almost sure I'd seen the face. But till this moment I confess I didn't recognise her, though from time to time I felt sure I'd seen her before. I wonder——"

He broke off, with a frown of annoyance and perplexity on his face. His wife knew what he meant.

"You wonder what she wants here?" she said significantly. "Well, so do I. I can't help thinking it is a very strange thing to do to sneak back into the house without making herself known, and I shall be very much surprised if we are not made to regret her reappearance!"

Sir Robert, who was not at all quick of perception, being an absent-minded, mild-natured man, wholly without suspicion or mistrust, looked more perplexed than ever.

"Why should we regret it?" he said. "She has grown into a most charming woman, gentle, sympathetic, and very clever and kind. I cannot even now realise that such a woman has grown out of the shy, lanky, white-faced girl who fell off the bicycle. I can't see anything wrong about her coming; and since I didn't recognise her I don't see why she should have felt it necessary to remind me who she was. She made no attempt at disguise, you know. I feel ashamed of my own stupidity in having forgotten her name."

The fact was that Rhoda Pembury's first appearance at the Mill-house was made at a time when the baronet, very much in love with Lady Sarah, was not in a condition to receive vivid impressions of any other person.

Lady Sarah brought him back to her point.

"Doesn't it seem to you strange that she should have said nothing to you about—about what happened here on the night she went away?"

Sir Robert's brow clouded.

"She has too much tact," he said, "to refer to anything so disagreeable."

"Oh yes, she has tact enough," retorted his wife with vivacity. "I hate to have to refer to this horrid subject, dear, but I warn you that I mistrust this girl. I think it most mysterious that it should have been impossible to get at her when she was wanted at the inquest, but that she should turn up here in this mysterious fashion ten years later, and worm herself into your confidence in the absence of your wife."

Sir Robert was still too much under the influence of his wife, on those rare occasions when she took the trouble to fascinate him again, not to be impressed by what she said. Nevertheless his gratitude to Rhoda, modified though it was by shame at his own forgetfulness, was strong enough to make him feel bound to stand up for her.

"I can't think there is any harm in her," he said gently. "What is it you mean to suggest?"

Lady Sarah gave a little enigmatic shrug.

"Oh, I don't suggest anything. Only don't, like the unsuspicious, kind-hearted old goose you are, trust her with too many of your secrets. That's all."

"Secrets! Why, I haven't any."

Lady Sarah laughed.

"Well then, don't encourage her to confide to you too many of *hers*!" she said, as, at the sound of the dinner gong, she tucked her little hand affectionately within her husband's arm and led him away to the dining-room.

Rhoda was waiting in the hall, having been apprised that she was expected to join them at dinner. During Lady Sarah's absence Sir Robert had dined alone, and she had, by Caryl's earnest request, dined in the room adjoining his bedroom, with the door open so that he might see her from his little bed.

In the first glance she exchanged with Sir Robert, Rhoda was shrewd enough to see that the ingratiating Lady Sarah had made mischief for her. Sir Robert was, indeed, more ashamed of his own obtuseness in not having recognised in the accomplished woman the half-fledged girl of ten years before, than imbued with his wife's suspicions of her. But what she had told him was enough to cause some alteration in his manner, and poor Rhoda felt the difference keenly.

Sir Robert had a horror of anything that recalled the murder of Langton, or the disagreeable rumours which had ensued. And the consequence was that during dinner he was taciturn and appeared almost morose, so that the conversation was left almost entirely to Lady Sarah and Rhoda.

When the ladies left the room he remained in the dining-room, but Lady Sarah, who was just as sweet as ever to Rhoda, excused herself from another *tête-à-tête* with the girl by saying that she knew her husband was sulking about something, and that she must go and have it out with him.

When Sir Robert, therefore, left the dining-room to join the ladies in the drawing-room, he found himself intercepted by Lady Sarah, who, sliding her hand along his sleeve in her most caressing manner, told him she wanted a talk with him, and led him off to his study.

Sir Robert had been married long enough to the capricious beauty to know that a raid of this kind always had its object. As soon, therefore, as they had reached the large and lofty apartment known as the study, he gently withdrew his arm, and placing an easy chair for her, threw himself into another, and said, not unkindly, but with an air of resignation:

"Well, and what is it you want now, my dear?"

Lady Sarah laughed with a very pretty appearance of confusion.

"Now, that's unkind," she said. "I'm sure I don't want anything but the pleasure of seeing how well and happy you look. I think, Bertie, it suits you for me to be away!"

He shrugged his shoulders slightly.

"I have to get used to it, don't I? Well, and now what is it that has brought you here to-night?"

"Won't you believe, then, that I'm anxious to have one of our nice little talks, after being all this time away?"

She crossed her feet, threw herself back in her chair, and putting one pretty little white jewelled hand on each arm of her chair, smiled at him bewitchingly.

It was impossible to resist her, and Sir Robert put one of his own hands upon one of hers.

"My dear, it's always a pleasure for me to talk to you," he said.

Lady Sarah gave a pretty little sigh.

"That's better," she said. "And you know, Bertie, if I do have to ask you for things, and of course I have to very often, it's only because you're rich, and I'm poor, and because I've nobody to go to but you, when I want money."

Sir Robert had withdrawn his hand, but he could not help a little amusement at the neatness with which she had come back to the important point.

"Of course it's perfectly natural and right that you should come to me for money, and as long as I have it I always give it you, don't I?"

Out of her half shut eyes she threw at him a reproachful glance. "You have plenty," she said plaintively.

"And I think I may truly say, dear," replied he, in the gentlest of voices, "that as long as I have plenty you have plenty too."

Lady Sarah sat up quickly.

"I haven't any now," she said. "I've come back without a cent! Look here. That's my very last sovereign!"

And opening her great brown eyes with a charming plaintiveness, she turned inside out a gold chain bag studded with pearls, which she wore suspended round her neck at the end of a very long chain, and displayed in triumph the solitary coin.

She was shrewd enough not to like the expression she saw on her husband's face. Yet it was in the kindest of voices that he said:

"Well, dear, give me your bills, and I will settle them for you."

But this did not happen to be what Lady Sarah wanted. She frowned petulantly.

"No, I'd rather have the money to settle them myself," she said.

He shook his head.

"I gave you plenty of money to go away with. But I must see the bills now."

"Why?"

He hesitated.

"Well, my dear, you are just a little extravagant, aren't you?"

She shrugged her shoulders.

"Am I?" she asked flippantly. "What *is* being extravagant? Is it buying new clothes when the old ones are worn out? Or is it," and she cast a glance, which was full of sly, mischievous humour, at her husband's grave face, "is it making an enormous collection of pictures at fabulous prices, and of antiques which may or may not be genuine, without being able to say whether, twenty years hence, they will have gone up in value, or down?"

Sir Robert winced.

"At any rate my pictures are a better investment than your frocks," he said: "but we won't quarrel about that. Ladies love pretty things, and the prettier the lady the more she loves them. I recognise that and I submit. So let me have the bills, and I'll pay them."

A furtive look of fear came into her face and died out again, and then she said:

"It's very good of you, Bertie, but I really do want some money for myself too, money to spend as I like, to waste, perhaps. Won't you let me have a couple of hundred to do as I like with?"

Sir Robert shook his head with decision.

"It's more than I can do just now, dear," he said. "Twenty pounds is the very utmost I can manage apart from the milliner's bills, which, I suppose, will not be light."

An angry light flashed out of her beautiful dark eyes. Sir Robert was the last man to be mistrustful or suspicious, but even he found a vague fear intruding into his mind when he noted the seriousness of her displeasure.

"Do you lose much money at bridge?" he asked quite suddenly.

She lost colour a little, but answered contemptuously:

"At bridge! No, of course not. I hate it, for one thing, and when I have to play I always take care not to lose much."

But Sir Robert's suspicions once roused were not easily laid.

"Do you gamble on the Stock Exchange?" he asked abruptly.

A look of genuine horror appeared in her eyes.

"I think I would as soon play pitch-and-toss!" she answered lightly.

His tone became more imperative:

"Do you bet on horses, or what? The money must go somewhere."

Again there was that same furtive look, but again she treated the question with hilarious contempt.

"Of course I don't do any of those things. However, if you won't trust me with a little money, I suppose I must submit. Never mind me and my poor little wants now. Let us have a chat about you and your pleasures. What have you been buying while I've been away? Some nice pictures? Some queer old china figures? Some real bargains in Chippendale chairs at twenty-five guineas a-piece? Come, let's take a walk through the gallery, and you shall show me the very latest arrivals."

Whether he believed in her interest or not, or whether he was glad that her importunities had ceased, Sir Robert was quite ready to show off his latest acquisition.

"I've got some lovely old French tapestries," he said, "that even you will admire, little Vandal that you are." He felt in his pockets and then exclaimed: "Oh, I haven't got the key of the gallery. Miss Pembury has charge of it now, for she's begun to make me a catalogue, and she is in there every morning before anybody else is up."

"Ah!" said Lady Sarah sharply.

Sir Robert looked at her quickly, but she would give no explanation of what was in her mind, and the expedition to the gallery was given up for that evening.

CHAPTER VI.
JACK ROTHERFIELD

NOBODY would have supposed, to judge by Lady Sarah's attitude to Rhoda, that any suspicion or mistrust of her had ever entered her pretty head.

On the contrary, she went out of her way to be charming to her boy's companion, openly congratulating herself on having provided him with such an amiable friend, and told Rhoda, with merry laughter, that she considered herself a most magnanimous person not to be jealous of such a formidable rival.

"Who would ever have thought that the thin, pale girl with the colourless hair would be transformed into—you?" she cried, "with your stately walk and dignified figure! You make me look so small, and so frivolous and empty-headed, that I shall end by being jealous of you with my own husband as well as my boy!"

Rhoda frowned painfully.

"I don't like to hear you say those things even in fun. Caryl looks upon me just as he would upon a nurse who was kind to him. He speaks of you with bated breath, as if you were a goddess. And it's the same with Sir Robert. All I can do is to make myself useful, and I have to work hard to keep my hold upon both of them; I have to keep a smile always ready for little Caryl and to indulge his whims; to keep my place in his heart I have to be always working, working hard. As for Sir Robert, I'm afraid his appreciation of me is confined to my capacity for making out his handwriting, and his admiration is given only to my beautiful capitals, and not to me. If I thought that you meant that I presumed upon my position——"

"But I don't, I don't, I don't!" cried Lady Sarah briskly. "I'm unfeignedly thankful for what you have done for both of them, and there never was in this world a person less capable of jealousy than I. But you are too modest. For I see Sir Robert lets you have the key of his gallery. I'm sure he'd rather die than trust it to me."

Rhoda's fair face became suffused with a hot blush.

"I won't let him give it me again," she said quickly.

Lady Sarah put a peremptory little hand upon her arm.

"Yes, yes, you will," she said. "You are much more to be trusted than either Sir Robert or I. For he is so absent-minded that he might leave it in a shop in payment for a postage stamp, while I am so dreadfully careless that I should certainly leave it sticking in the door. Now come, don't be cross, but put on your hat and I'll take you to the Priory with me and introduce you to my old mother. She's rather a dear when you come to know her well, though you may find her uninteresting at first."

Rhoda would have made excuses, but Lady Sarah was accustomed to have her own way, and upon the whole Rhoda was not displeased to have an opportunity of seeing Vale Priory and its occupants.

And so, before mid-day, she and Lady Sarah got into the motor-car, and after climbing the long hill out of Dourville, and down the other side of it into the vale, they reached the pretty, old-fashioned mansion which had been in the family of the Marquis of Eridge for a couple of centuries.

The house was in almost every respect a great contrast to Sir Robert's residence, as altered by the taste of Lady Sarah. It was old, it was shabby, it was not in the best of repair. But there was some charm about it, as there always is about a house which has been lived in by refined people for two or three generations. It bore the stamp of its owners, and although these were not remarkable in any way, Lady Sarah with her brilliant beauty having indeed been regarded as a "sport" and a surprise to those who knew the stock from which she came, there was something pleasing in the atmosphere of the old place, something of dignity in the occupants of the house, something of beauty in the dwelling itself.

The river flowed within a hundred yards of the garden front of the house, and on the other side the ground sloped gently upwards, a smooth expanse of grass, dotted by well-grown trees.

In a low armchair near the large window of the largest drawing-room sat the Marchioness of Eridge, a tall, massive woman with grey hair and that look of vacuous and vague displeasure with things in general which results from lofty pretensions and the possession of means inadequate to maintain them.

Her two unmarried daughters, both older than Lady Sarah, and altogether lacking in their sister's brilliant good looks, were working, the one with her knitting, the other with some sort of fancy work, at another window.

Lady Sarah, followed more sedately by Rhoda, came in like a whirlwind, and stirred the quiet ladies into something like life as if by magic.

"What, Philippa! Aileen! Both indoors! On a morning like this! How can you?"

Her mother smiled, the two other ladies looked up with a little flush of pleasure in their pale faces, as Rhoda was introduced to them, in a highly complimentary fashion, by Lady Sarah, who expatiated upon her goodness to Caryl, and incidentally mentioned that she was the heroine of the bicycle accident of ten years before.

There was great interest at this, and Rhoda saw curiosity in the three faces. But Lady Sarah skimmed lightly away from that subject and told of her own travels and of her future plans.

"I'm going over to the chrysanthemum show at Canterbury to-morrow," she said. "And I want to know whether one of you would like to come too. Jack is coming to-night, and he will take us."

Lady Eridge drew herself up.

"Jack Rotherfield!" exclaimed she. "Do you really mean that he's coming again? Why, he's always at your house. Does Sir Robert approve?"

There was a little spot of red colour in Lady Sarah's cheeks as she said quickly:

"Why shouldn't he approve? He was Jack's guardian once. And now, though it's nine years ago, naturally they feel the same towards each other still."

"He doesn't come to see Robert, for he only comes when you are at home," said Lady Eridge, in some displeasure. "People must notice it, and I am surprised that Robert doesn't notice it himself."

"I hope you won't put any ridiculous notions into Robert's head, mama," said Lady Sarah. "Jack and I have always been the best of friends, and it would distress me very much if anything were said which would make it difficult for him to feel at home in Robert's house."

"Did you see him at all while you were away?" asked Lady Eridge.

But Lady Sarah found it convenient not to hear the question. She was by this time talking to her sisters, who were full of inquiries as to what she had been doing with herself during her stay abroad, and what she had done with Minnie.

Minnie was in town with some cousins, Lady Sarah said. She was evidently displeased at her mother's rebuke, and she did not stay very long.

Lady Eridge, who was very gracious to Rhoda, invited her to come to tea on the following day.

"It was I," she explained to the girl, "who suggested to my daughter that she should try to find some nice lady to be a companion to poor little Caryl, and I should have called to see you before now, Miss Pembury, but that my daughters and I have been staying in Yorkshire ever since you came."

Rhoda, who was much pleased at her reception, but vaguely disturbed by something she had heard, thanked the marchioness, and left the house with Lady Sarah, who proceeded to explain to her that the quiet life led by the ladies of her family made them rather narrow and old-fashioned in their views.

"They think it shocking of me to be away from home so much," said she, "and they can't see that it is better that I should be home now and then in a good temper, than always here in a bad one."

Rhoda laughed, but said nothing. She perceived already that Sir Robert's dream of happiness with the woman he loved for his wife had failed of realisation.

It was in some perturbation of spirit that she awaited the arrival of that Jack Rotherfield who, as she suddenly remembered, had been certainly better loved by Lady Sarah before her marriage than was her own *fiancé*.

She scarcely knew what she feared, or if she did, she did not like to put her fears into shape. But the warning of the marchioness, coming so soon after her discovery that Lady Sarah's heart was not in her own home, was distressing to the loyal and straightforward girl.

Rhoda was on the terrace that afternoon with Caryl, when the sound of a male voice as well as that of Lady Sarah in the drawing-room attracted her attention.

"That's Jack!" said Caryl. "I thought he'd be here soon. He's always here when mama comes back."

Rhoda said nothing. But these words did not tend to make her more at ease. There came a hush in the voices when Caryl called out, and then Lady Sarah appeared at the drawing-room window.

A moment later the handsome face of Jack Rotherfield appeared over her shoulder.

He was looking as merry as ever, and, after turning to say a few words to him, Lady Sarah came out and re-introduced him to Rhoda, whom he greeted with as much apparent pleasure as if she had been an old friend.

It was quite impossible not to like him, for he had as much personal fascination as Lady Sarah herself; and it was impossible not to be struck by the fact, when brought thus face to face with them together, that they would have made a much better-matched pair, with their common interest and their liveliness of temperament, than did frivolous, pleasure-loving Lady Sarah and her absent-minded and grave lord.

Caryl was sent upstairs with his nurse, against the wish of Rhoda, who was forced to stay to have tea with Lady Sarah and Jack.

They all entered the drawing-room together, and Lady Sarah asked Rhoda to pour out the tea. Then Jack Rotherfield came up to take a cup to Lady Sarah.

Rhoda turned to him with a smile as he held out his hand. Then Lady Sarah spoke to him and he turned for a moment, answering her. Rhoda, still holding the cup, glanced down at his hand, and perceived that across the back of it, extending from the one side to the other, was a distinct scar.

In an instant there flashed back into her mind the remembrance of the night when she left the Mill-house, of the struggle she had heard in the drawing-room, and of the hand she had seen in the moonlight, with the red mark of a cut across it.

Unable to restrain her feelings, she uttered a sharp cry.

"What's that?" she gasped, as she pointed to the scar.

CHAPTER VII.
THE SCARRED HAND

RHODA, with her eyes fixed on the scarred hand, did not see either of the faces turned towards her, did not catch the quick look exchanged between Jack Rotherfield and Lady Sarah, or note their rapid loss of colour.

It was quite a long time before anybody spoke. Then Lady Sarah, crossing the room slowly and with apparent carelessness, asked:

"What's the matter?"

Rhoda looked up, but there was a mist before her eyes; she said nothing, but rose unsteadily from her chair and took a couple of steps toward the window.

She was stopped, however, before she reached it, and found Lady Sarah's hand within her arm.

"Don't go away, Miss Pembury. Tell me, are you ill? What is it?"

The light bright voice was unchanged. But Rhoda, still breathing heavily, though the mist seemed to be clearing away, glanced quickly at her, and perceived that she was still of a deadly pallor.

"Let me go," whispered the girl. "I—I'm not well—I—I feel faint."

"I'll take you into the garden. Jack, bring out a chair, and find a sunshade."

Rhoda shuddered at the name, and looked round. Jack Rotherfield was pale also, although he tried to carry it off in an unconcerned manner. Rhoda would have escaped, but she was firmly held, and made to sit in the verandah, while her companions stood one on each side of her.

Rhoda had noticed, without being sufficiently herself to take in the significance of the fact, that there had been a short colloquy between them. Now Lady Sarah suddenly seized Jack's right hand, and holding it close under Rhoda's face, said:

"This was what shocked you, wasn't it? The mark on his poor hand? I'll tell you all about it."

Rhoda bowed her head. She knew that she was going to hear a trumped-up story, but she had to listen. What the real truth was as to Jack Rotherfield's connection with the tragedy that took place at the Mill-house ten years before she did not yet know, but that it was not what she was going to hear she was quite sure.

"Do you remember—I'm awfully sorry to have to remind you of it, for it's an unpleasant subject, but I must—Do you remember the night you went away from here all those years ago?"

"Yes," said Rhoda below her breath.

"And do you know that, on that very night, the poor butler, Langton, was found lying dead in the drawing-room?"

Rhoda bowed her head.

"Well, the next day the place was in a dreadful state, everybody excited and half-crazy. We were all following out the track of the burglar who had got in and murdered the poor man. And standing by the drawing-room window, with Sir Robert and me, Jack, opening it quickly, thrust his hand through the glass, and cut it right open. I fainted. Coming so soon after the ghastly discovery we had made, it made me quite ill. Sir Robert carried me to the sofa, and the doctor, who was in the house with the police, bound up Jack's hand first, and then came up and attended to me, and then mama took me home!"

Rhoda bowed her head in silence. Lady Sarah waited for some sort of an apology for her behaviour, but she made none. After rather a long pause, during which Rhoda suddenly looked up and perceived a stealthy interchange of looks of alarm between the other two, she got up and murmured something about going back to Caryl.

"Not yet," said Lady Sarah, "you are not well enough yet to be teased by the boy. Sit still, and I will bring your tea out to you. Jack, fetch Miss Pembury's cup, and mine too, there's a good boy. And then go and ask Sir Robert if he will come and have some too."

Jack hesitated, but she gave him another look, and he obeyed.

Within five minutes Rhoda was sitting with her tea-cup in her hand, Lady Sarah was beside her, and Jack was returning along the terrace with Sir Robert.

When she was alone with the other lady, Rhoda seized the opportunity to say:

"I'm sorry I cried out as I did, but——"

She could not go on, and after a pause, Lady Sarah finished her sentence for her.

"The sight of a scar or wound distresses you. I understand. Some people are very sensitive to anything like that. But it's not really painful now, you know. At the moment it happened I thought it must be, for it looked so dreadful. But even then I think perhaps I suffered more at the sight of the wound than Jack did himself."

"Yes."

Lady Sarah turned quickly to her husband, who was now in sight.

"Bertie," she said, "Tell Miss Pembury how Jack cut his hand."

Rhoda rose quickly from her chair.

"Oh, no," she said hastily, "I don't want to hear any more, really."

But Lady Sarah insisted.

"You must," she said, with peremptoriness, which betrayed the importance she attached to the apparently small matter.

Sir Robert was not at all pleased at his wife's question, recalling an episode in his life which he would fain have forgotten.

"He put his hand through a window," he said briefly, "and the mark shows still, as I dare say you have noticed, Miss Pembury."

Rhoda said "Yes" under her breath, but there was still upon her face a dazed look of incredulity which irritated Lady Sarah.

The girl took the first opportunity of escaping upstairs, but she was in no state to amuse little Caryl, so she hastened to her own room, locked herself in, and sitting down, breathless and trembling, on a chair near the window, gave herself up to her distress, her doubts and her fears.

What did it mean? What could it mean but one thing?

There stood out clearly in her recollection the remembrance of the terrible night of her escape from the Mill-house, and the sight of the moonlight streaming on the hand with the red wound across it. That the hand she had seen that night was the hand of Jack Rotherfield she was quite sure. Her impression of the red mark she had seen that night was so strong, that nothing would have shaken her in this conviction. True, it was difficult to understand the story she had just heard, and wholly impossible to believe that Sir Robert was not telling the truth when he said he had seen the hand gashed by the broken window.

But Rhoda, who mistrusted Lady Sarah as strongly as she trusted her husband, thought that the clever little lady, who had certainly succeeded in throwing dust in Sir Robert's eyes before her marriage, was quite capable of having deceived him by a trick. How it was managed the girl could not quite understand; but she felt sure that Jack, having been concerned in the death of Langford, was the man with the wounded hand whom she saw on his way upstairs; and she believed that the wound had been received in a struggle with the poor butler, and that, in order to avoid bringing suspicion upon himself, the young man had been artful enough to conceal his injury until the following day, when, taking an opportunity when there were several people present, he had thrust his wounded hand through the window as if by accident, and led those present to believe that the cut was freshly made.

Some such trick as this Rhoda felt sure had been played, but it sickened her to think that, in that case, Lady Sarah must have been a party to the stratagem, by which Jack shielded himself and deceived Sir Robert at the same time.

What was the whole truth concerning that night? Rhoda wondered.

It was now quite clear to her that, by accident or by design, it was Jack Rotherfield who caused the death of the butler. If it was an accident, why had he not told the truth about the night's events? If it was more than that, what was the reason of his quarrel with the servant?

Certain dark suggestions did pass through her mind, but she would not encourage them. The thing was a mystery, an ugly mystery, and the ugliest part of it undoubtedly was that Lady Sarah was evidently in the confidence of the young man, and that he and she were still engaged together in practising a deception upon the lady's husband.

Rhoda shuddered at the thought.

If Lady Sarah could deceive her trusting and indulgent husband to the extent of keeping such a secret from his ears for ten years, how was it possible to believe that she did not deceive him even farther?

The best thing to be said for the volatile beauty that her friendship with Jack Rotherfield was perfectly open, that he was constantly the guest of her husband, who certainly had no doubts of the loyalty either of his wife or of his late ward.

Why, therefore, Rhoda told herself, should she worry herself about the matter, since Sir Robert did not?

But argue as she might, she knew that there was more in the story than had become known; and while refusing to believe that even the artful Lady Sarah could go the length of wronging the man who trusted her so nobly she knew that the wife was lacking in sterling loyalty, and that, while she might be, and probably was, careful of herself and of her position, she bestowed more confidence upon Jack Rotherfield, if she did not more affection, than she gave to her own husband.

The knowledge which had come to her so suddenly that day, the conviction that she had in her hands now the clue to the mystery of the murder, made Rhoda so uneasy that she felt sure she would not be able to remain long in the household.

How could she go from husband to wife, and back again, with a light enough heart and a free conscience, when she was burdened, as she now was, with part, at least, of such an important secret?

Would Lady Sarah wish her to remain at the Mill-house? Rhoda thought not. It could not be pleasant to the proud little mistress of the house to feel that there was some one under the same roof who knew so much as Rhoda did, and she could not fail to look upon the girl as a spy, and to wonder whether she would keep to herself what she knew.

Rhoda felt that she must prepare for an early departure.

She was very sorry; for she had already attached herself deeply to little Caryl, while her feeling for the grave, gentle Sir Robert, having lost the quality of girlish enthusiasm which she had cherished for him ten years before, had become deeper, more pathetic, in the knowledge that he was not being treated as he had every right to be by the woman he loved so loyally and indulged in such a princely fashion.

It was in a very nervous condition that Rhoda rejoined the family at dinner that evening. She expected to find a difference in Lady Sarah's manner towards her, but she was surprised indeed to find what that difference proved to be.

If she had been kind before, charming, merry, amiable, now Lady Sarah was infinitely more fascinating, more bent on making herself agreeable to her son's companion.

With the most tender concern she asked after the headache which had been Rhoda's excuse for leaving them that afternoon. Most sweetly she insisted that the girl was devoting herself too closely to her care of Caryl, and that, in order to get some relaxation, she must go to-morrow to the Chrysanthemum Show.

"Oh, no, it would leave me no time," objected Rhoda. "You know Lady Eridge has asked me to tea at the Priory to-morrow afternoon."

"Never mind. You shall go to the Show, too, and, as one of my sisters will be with me, I will drop you both at the Priory as we come back."

It was of no use to attempt to thwart Lady Sarah; she never heeded any objection to her plans; and Sir Robert, smiling, told Rhoda so when she still kept up an attempt at protest.

Jack Rotherfield seemed quite untroubled by the discovery Rhoda had made that afternoon. He chatted so gaily, was so charming, so merry, and babbled on about things in general with so much easy gaiety that Sir Robert, who delighted in his conversation, was more animated than Rhoda had ever seen him before.

She was the only member of the party who was grave, pre-occupied and unhappy. She knew that Lady Sarah and Jack noticed this, and that Sir Robert was the only person present who failed to observe the depression from which she was suffering.

Later in the evening, when she would have escaped upstairs, she was detained and made to play and sing. She accompanied Jack Rotherfield in his songs, receiving his thanks and compliments upon her skill with coldness and shrinking which she did her best, not very successfully, to hide.

When she went upstairs she had a good cry. Sir Robert, the one of all the rest whom she liked and respected, had been slightly conscious, towards the end of the evening, of a difference in her manner, and had been perplexed and slightly displeased by it, while the two persons who overwhelmed her with civility and kindness were those from whom she would have preferred to receive as little attention as possible.

Truly her position was growing difficult, and she was sure that before long it would be impossible.

However, on the following day she recovered her spirits a little, feeling so sure that she would not stay long at the Mill-house that she determined to enjoy her time there as much as she could, and to trouble herself as little as possible about those causes of uneasiness which she could not help.

After a pleasant morning with Caryl, she was whirled off to Canterbury in the motor-car with Lady Sarah, Jack Rotherfield, and Lady Aileen, enjoyed herself in spite of her own wishes, and was landed with Lady Aileen at the door of the Priory in time for tea.

Lady Eridge was most gracious, and so were her two daughters, while the marquis, who came in quietly while they were all chatting round the little fire, without which the marchioness always felt chilly when the sun went down, was kind and good-natured, asked Rhoda the same questions two or three times over, and being rather deaf, always failed to catch the answers.

It was not until Lady Eridge had found an opportunity to speak to the visitor apart from the rest, that she broached the subject which Rhoda felt must have been in her thoughts all the time.

"And so you like the life at the Mill-house?" she began, after she had looked round nervously, and put out one waxlike hand to try to detect the bugbear of her sheltered life, "a draught."

"Oh, yes, I like it very much. They are all kind to me, and I'm as fond of Caryl as if I'd lived with him for years."

"And I hear you are a great help to Sir Robert?"

"Oh, no, not a great help. I'm interested in his work, and so grateful to him for what he did for me ten years ago in saving my life, that I'm most eager to do anything I can. It isn't much, of course."

"You are doing the things that my daughter ought to do herself," said Lady Eridge.

"Do you mean that I ought not to do them?" asked Rhoda anxiously.

But the old lady answered quite eagerly:

"By no means. I am hoping that she will see now just what she ought to be doing herself, and that she may be induced to take up her duties," said Lady Eridge. "As it is, she spends far too much time away from home. If she found an interest in her husband's pleasures she would not find so much temptation to go abroad and to town."

"Somehow it doesn't seem natural to expect her to take an interest in making catalogues, and work of that sort," said Rhoda. "She is so brilliant, so—so lively, that I'm sure she would look upon such occupations as too dry for her."

"Since they are not too dry for you, why should they be for her?"

"Well, I was always a staid, quiet person, not a bit like Lady Sarah."

The marchioness looked at her keenly, and Rhoda blushed.

"Do you think," suggested the girl in a hesitating manner, "that it is right for me to do what I am doing? It seemed so natural, when I first came, and found Sir Robert rather helpless in the midst of the notes that he couldn't read, to take up the easy and pleasant work of helping him, that I fell into it without, perhaps, considering whether I was not taking too much upon myself. Now I begin already to realise that my position is a little difficult, and to wonder whether I ought to go away."

The old lady laid her hand impressively upon the girl's arm.

"No, my dear, you are to stay," she said earnestly. "I was delighted to see you yesterday, and again to-day, and to believe more and more that we have found in you just the link which has been wanting. You have a mission in that household, Miss Pembury, a delicate one perhaps, but one that I am sure you will perform in the most efficient manner."

"Oh, no, no," cried Rhoda. "I am not so ambitious. And indeed I would much rather retire into the background altogether."

Lady Eridge interrupted her.

"You will not hesitate, I am sure," she said, "to give up your own wishes when you realise what a useful office you could perform if you could succeed in drawing these two nearer together."

"I don't think you quite realise, Lady Eridge," replied Rhoda earnestly, "the difficulty of interfering in any way between husband and wife."

"I shouldn't call it interference."

"But that's what it must come to," persisted Rhoda. "And the task requires a great deal more tact and cleverness than I possess. Lady Sarah is cleverer than I am, and she is more likely to do what she pleases with me, than I am to make her do anything she doesn't care to do of her own free will."

But obstinacy was a trait which Lady Sarah had inherited from her mother, and the Marchioness went on:

"I don't want you to preach to her, or anything of that kind. It is by example that I want you to lead her back to her duty."

Rhoda shook her head.

"Indeed you're asking too much of me, Lady Eridge, and I couldn't undertake anything of the sort. My only fear is that I shall soon find my present modest position in the household too difficult for me, and that I shall have to go away."

"Why is it difficult?"

Rhoda hesitated. Not for worlds would she have betrayed a suspicion of the real difficulties which beset her path, of the mystery of which she now had an inkling, and of which she feared to obtain further knowledge. How could she suggest to the marchioness that Jack Rotherfield was, if not actually the murderer of poor Langton, at least concerned actively in his death, and that Lady Sarah appeared to have been, if not an accomplice, at least an accessory after the fact?

"How do Sir Robert and Mr. Rotherfield get on together?" asked Lady Eridge as if carelessly, though Rhoda knew well the thought that was in her mind.

"Quite well. Sir Robert is very fond of him, and I have never seen him laugh or talk so much as he did last night at dinner when Mr. Rotherfield was there."

"Yes. He is a most amusing companion, I must admit. But I think he is too flippant and too extravagant to be a safe friend for a young married woman. You will perhaps be surprised, Miss Pembury, that I speak to you so openly. But you have been initiated into the family circumstances, and you must have noticed for yourself that there is not that sympathy between my daughter and her husband that there ought to be, and that she is too much inclined to spend her time in frivolous pleasures. She is too extravagant, and I think that Mr. Rotherfield encourages her in it. Certainly she seems to grow more and more wasteful in money matters."

"Wouldn't she listen to you, if you were to speak to her on the subject? I certainly could not," said Rhoda.

Lady Eridge shrugged her shoulders.

"Unfortunately it is impossible to influence her by preaching. That is why I am hoping so much from your example."

"You must not hope, Lady Eridge. If Lady Sarah were to have the least suspicion that I was to be held up to her as a pattern, my life would at once become unendurable. And I should be sorry to have to go, for Caryl's sake."

Lady Eridge leaned back with a sigh.

"I shall persist in hoping," she said gently. "And in believing that you may be working for good without your own knowledge."

When Rhoda went away she was oppressed by a new sense of responsibility and uneasiness. New difficulties seemed to be cropping up at every step. The idea of her influencing the wilful, artful wife of Sir Robert was laughable, or would have been so if she had not felt that there was something pitiful in the anxiety of the mother to bring wholesome influences to bear upon her self-willed, extravagant daughter.

Of course Rhoda knew that she could do nothing, unless indeed she could contrive to put in a word of warning to Sir Robert to tighten his hold a little on his erratic wife.

But how was she to dare to intervene?

She was walking more and more slowly, weighed down by her anxieties, when she heard rapid footsteps behind her, and then her name uttered in Jack Rotherfield's voice:

"Miss Pembury!"

The next moment he had caught her up, and was laughing down merrily into her face. In spite of all that she knew and all that she guessed, Rhoda found it impossible to be as stiff and cold to him as she wished. How could she retain her belief that he was guilty of manslaughter, if not of actual murder, when he could laugh so merrily, and speak so light-heartedly, that she could scarcely believe the man of thirty to be more than a boy still?

"I've been tearing after you for three fields and a half, and now I'm completely blown and can only pant!" he cried, with an affectation of laboured breathing which hardly interfered with his volubility. "I've been hanging about to escort you back to the Mill-house. I knew you'd take the short cut through the fields, and it's hardly safe or pleasant for a young lady so late as this."

"Oh, I can take care of myself," said Rhoda.

She was rather dry of manner, and she would not even thank him, though his amiability made her feel ungracious.

He assumed an appearance of intense dejection.

"So you're one of the strong-minded sisterhood," he said dolefully. "Now I shouldn't have thought it of you. It isn't what one would have expected you to turn out, when I knew you first, ten years ago."

Rhoda was silent. She looked at him cautiously out of the corners of her eyes, and saw in his the anxiety she had expected to see. He wanted to "pump" her, she knew, concerning the extent of her information as to the doings of the night of the death of Langton.

"You were as timid as a hare, a little shy girl with big eyes! But you were always nice to me then, much nicer than you are now. Why aren't you as nice to me as you used to be?"

"I don't think I quite know what you mean by 'nice,'" Rhoda answered. "There must be a difference, I suppose, between the manner of a girl of seventeen and that of a woman of twenty-seven."

"You haven't taken a dislike to me for anything?"

She could scarcely repress a shudder, but she answered hastily:

"Of course not. Why should I?"

"I fancied that you had though, without any reason," persisted he. "I thought it rather ungrateful of you, because I was so awfully glad to meet you again."

"Thank you."

"Glad too, for Lady Sarah's sake and Sir Robert's, because they're so pleased with your devotion to Caryl, and with the way you've dropped into the family interests."

To Rhoda's great joy they had reached the high road, and she was able to escape him by getting on a tram-car which would take her into Dourville. He got in too, but there were other passengers inside, so that he had to make his conversation more general and less embarrassing.

But she could not help fancying, when she got home and thought over their walk, that he had had something to say which he had had no opportunity of saying, and she resolved to do her best to avoid him for the future.

As she came to that conclusion, she became conscious, to her own surprise, that in spite of his merry eyes, his liveliness and his charm, in spite of her belief that his guilt in the matter of Langton's death could not have been that of murder, she was more afraid of Jack Rotherfield than she had ever been of any man in her life before.

And she realised that in the rare moments when she got a glimpse of his features in repose, there were lines in his face which should not have been there, lines which indicated that, under all his surface gaiety and charm, there was all the hardness and the capacity for cruelty of an utterly selfish nature.

CHAPTER VIII.
THE MISSING SNUFF-BOXES

WHEN she reached home, Rhoda was met in the hall by Sir Robert. His usually placid countenance was disturbed, and a horrible suspicion flashed through her mind, as he came straight towards her, that he was going to ask her some awkward questions about Lady Sarah or Mr. Rotherfield.

Advancing towards her so eagerly that it was clear he had been waiting for her, he said:

"Oh, Miss Pembury, I'm so glad you've come back. I've been waiting for you this half hour." Then, perceiving that she grew white, and was evidently alarmed, he added with a rather forced smile: "Don't look so frightened. It's nothing serious, at least nothing very serious. This way, please."

Trembling and cold, Rhoda followed him into the study, where he shut the door and made her sit down before he would come to the point.

"Now I don't want you to worry yourself, but can you tell me whether we moved the snuff-boxes from their place in the third specimen table from the end of the gallery?"

Deadly pale, Rhoda drew a long breath.

"No," she replied hoarsely. "They were there this morning; I'm sure of it."

Sir Robert frowned in distress.

"I thought so," he said. "Well, come with me now, and you will see that the three best are missing."

"Oh!" broke from her lips in such a tone of distress that he put his hand kindly on her shoulder.

"Don't worry yourself about it," said he. "They'll turn up all right, I've no doubt. But, if you don't mind, we'll just go into the gallery together and make sure of the fact of their disappearance."

Scarcely able to walk, so overpowered was she by a nameless dread, Rhoda accompanied him along the passage which led to the gallery. Since Rhoda had undertaken so much work for him in connection with his treasures, the baronet had had a set of duplicate keys made, so that, while he kept the one in his own possession, Rhoda had charge of the other. She had been rather reluctant to receive this mark of confidence, not feeling quite sure that Lady Sarah might not resent it. But Sir Robert had insisted, and she had found it a convenience to go into the gallery when she had a spare moment, to go on with the work she had undertaken.

Now, however, she began to wish with all her heart that she had not undertaken this responsibility, perceiving that she might have involved herself in a serious difficulty.

Quickly and in silence she followed Sir Robert, who opened the door of the gallery with his own key, turned on the electric light, and led the way to the end, where, in a glass-covered specimen table, it was his habit to keep about a dozen old snuff-boxes of exquisite workmanship, the aggregate value of which was some thousands of pounds.

He stopped short in front of the table, and Rhoda looked down at it. One, two, three of the treasures were missing, and the choice had been a most judicious one, for the three boxes which had disappeared were all of gold, all painted by celebrated artists, and all mounted with jewels.

"You see the three have gone," said he, while Rhoda stood beside him, unable to utter a word. "And the rest have been so carefully arranged that they look, at first sight, as if none were missing."

"They've been stolen," said Rhoda hoarsely.

"That's what I think. Now the question is when, how, and by whom? In the first place whose keys have been got hold of—yours or mine? Mine have never been out of my pocket or my hand all day. What about yours?"

Rhoda uttered a low cry.

"I left them in my room, in the pocket of the dress I wore this morning, when I changed it for this one to go to the flower show," she answered, brokenly.

"Some one has perhaps got at them. Would you mind going up to see whether they are still in the pocket of your dress?"

His tone was just as kind and gentle as ever; but to Rhoda, who was suffering an agony of mortification at what she thought he must consider her carelessness, fled along the gallery without a word. But his kind voice checked her before she reached the door. He was calling to her quite gently:

"Miss Pembury! My dear Miss Pembury, don't take this so much to heart. I've no doubt the keys will turn up. But even if they should not, pray, pray understand that you are in no way to blame."

"Oh yes, I am, oh yes, I am. I ought to have taken them with me!"

"Not at all. I often leave my own keys in the pocket of my coat, and there was not the least reason for you to think yours were any less safe. And remember, we don't yet know whether it was your keys that were used. A lock may be picked, you know."

But, though Rhoda thanked him and tried to hope, she was weighed down by the dreadful certainty that it was indeed her keys which had been used by the thief. And there flashed through her mind as she ran up the stairs a horrible vague dread that this theft might have been committed with the object of discrediting her with Sir Robert.

She flew along the corridor, locked herself in her room, and opening the door of her wardrobe, pulled out the dress with trembling hands, and felt in the pockets.

The keys were not there.

With a low cry, she put the dress back, and looked about the room in the vain hope that she might have dropped the keys somewhere while she was putting her dress away.

But it was hoping against hope, and at last she had to give up her search, and stealing out of her room, feeling as guilty as if she herself had been the thief, she went slowly back along the corridor and down the stairs, to the study.

"Come in," cried Sir Robert in his kind voice.

She could scarcely turn the handle of the door, and when she was inside the room, she could do nothing but utter whispered exclamations of distress.

The baronet laughed at her in the most reassuring manner, and pushed her gently into a chair.

"Don't behave like that, you silly, silly girl!" said he in a robust and reassuring voice. "I see what it is: you haven't found the keys. They're gone. Is that it?"

She bowed her head in assent.

"I'm quite, quite sure I put them in my pocket this morning, and that I didn't take them out again after I'd done my work in the gallery. Some one must have taken them out. Some one who knew where I kept them."

She sat up and stared at him almost fiercely.

The words distressed him, she saw.

"Do you think that perhaps they fell as you were either putting them in or taking them out again? Do you think it possible that you may have let them drop, and that they may have been picked up by one of the servants? I should hate to have to suspect any member of my household, but there are some who have not been here long, and one knows that some one must have taken the snuff-boxes."

"I should have heard them fall," said Rhoda uncertainly.

"Do you think there was a hole in your pocket?"

"No. I don't think so."

"Or that they may have slipped out on to the floor of your room?"

"I've hunted everywhere," said Rhoda.

"Of course it is plain that the things have been stolen, and probably by means of your keys," said he. "But I would rather think that the keys had been picked up and that the finder yielded to a sudden temptation than that a deliberate plot was hatched to rob me by hunting in your pockets while you were away. That would be abominable, odious, unpardonable."

Sir Robert grew quite warm as he thought of such an act of treachery.

"I wonder if I did drop them," said Rhoda doubtfully. "But I really don't think it possible. I'm not so careless as all that," she went on piteously. "When I look upon it as such a high honour to have the keys at all."

She threw at Sir Robert a look so plaintive, so full of apology and despair that he could not help smiling, as he told her not to worry her head about it, but to be sure that everything would come right.

"If it is one of the young servants who has been tempted," said he, "I will try to get at him or her through the housekeeper, or by some other means, and to persuade him or her into restitution. So dry your eyes and go and dress for dinner, and try to forget all about this little *contretemps*."

With dumb gratitude in her eyes poor Rhoda stole upstairs again and shut herself once more in her room. She was heartbroken over the unhappy affair, and could not help considering herself to have failed in her duty as custodian.

As for the identity of the thief, she could not even make a reasonable guess. The household was a large one, there were members of it she had never even seen. As perhaps none of them knew that she had duplicate keys, except one or two of the upper servants who were wholly to be trusted, Rhoda began to ask herself whether Sir Robert's suggestion might not be a good one, that she had dropped the keys on to the soft carpet of the corridor as she came out of the study, instead of slipping them into her pocket.

In the meantime she would make sure that her pocket was really sound, as she supposed.

So she opened her wardrobe once more, and thrust her hand again into the pocket in which she usually carried the keys.

And the keys were there, not one missing. Rhoda pulled them out with a hand that was wet and trembling, and sat down on the nearest chair, sick at heart and cold with a strange, new fear.

CHAPTER IX.
RHODA'S WATCHFULNESS

THERE could no longer be any question that the theft of the snuff-boxes was deliberate, and moreover that it had been most carefully planned and cleverly carried out.

Who then was the thief?

Half ashamed of herself for her suspicions, Rhoda yet could not but feel that they all pointed in the same direction. And she shuddered at the thought that this plot had been made against herself, and that it was not robbery but slander which was the object of the thief.

Not one of the younger servants could possibly know anything about the duplicate keys; while the older ones were all incapable, whatever their knowledge might be, of using it against her or against their master.

Only one person besides Sir Robert himself was aware that she had a set of keys for the gallery, a large one to open the door, and smaller ones to open the cases and chests.

Only one person, she argued, would have had either the artfulness to conceive the robbery, or the nerve to carry it out.

Daring as her suspicion could not fail to seem, even to herself, Rhoda at once decided that the theft was the work of Lady Sarah, of whose secret animosity she was well assured.

And that its object was to discredit Rhoda by bringing upon her the suspicion of theft seemed to her, at first, equally certain.

What other explanation, indeed, could there be for such an act on the part of the over-indulged wife of a rich man? Rhoda did not know all that had passed, since Lady Sarah's return, between the baronet and his wife, and it did not occur to her that Lady Sarah could possibly be pressed for money. As for the ruinous extravagance of the beauty, of which Lady Eridge had spoken, however much she might wish to spend she appeared to have enough to gratify every wish and every whim.

Rhoda did not doubt that the next stage in the affair would be a gradual coolness on Sir Robert's part towards herself, and that soon she would learn, more or less explicitly, that her honesty was under suspicion.

In the meantime she dared not breathe a word of her own doubts to any one, but could only wait to be attacked.

What should she do in the meantime? To ask permission to go away would be to bring fresh odium upon herself, while to remain would expose her to the possibility of more suspicion.

Not unnaturally, poor Rhoda found, when the gong sounded for dinner, that her eyes were red, her face was swollen, and she was emphatically what women call "not fit to be seen." However, there was no help for it.

Downstairs she had to go, to endure as best she might the covert looks of Lady Sarah, and, of course, of Mr. Rotherfield, who, she did not doubt, would be in the secret of her discomfiture.

Nothing was said about her altered looks; Sir Robert gave her a kind and reassuring smile, from which she augured, with a ray of comfort, that he had not yet been induced to doubt her. But Lady Sarah and Jack Rotherfield did not appear to notice the change in her appearance, and, although the master of the house was not so lively as he usually was in the society of his late ward, his wife and Jack kept the conversation alive during dinner.

Rhoda would have escaped upstairs at once on leaving the dining-room, but Lady Sarah detained her, saying that they wanted her to play and sing for them again.

"Won't you excuse me to-night, Lady Sarah? Really, I'm not at all well," said Rhoda.

Lady Sarah pulled her down the stairs peremtorily.

"Nonsense," whispered she. "I know all about it. I know what's the matter. Only of course I couldn't allude to it before the servants. Come into the drawing-room and let us talk it over."

Trembling and reluctant, but unable to resist the wilful beauty, even though she hated her for her dissimilation and her treachery, Rhoda had to consent to a *tête-à-tête* which she would have given the world to avoid.

In to the brightly lighted apartment, therefore, which could scarcely be recognised as the old drawing-room where the unhappy Langton had met his death, Rhoda was dragged. Lady Sarah threw her down into the deep-seated settee near the fireplace, and pulling across the floor a high round stool, she seated herself upon it, embraced her knees like a child, and nodded gravely at the girl two or three times.

"Yes, I know all about it," she said. "Sir Robert told me. Some wretch has stolen three or four of Sir Robert's patch-boxes, and you and he thinks that your keys or his must have been got at. It's very unpleasant and uncomfortable, and I'm sorry for your sake. But not so much for any other. It will be a lesson to Sir Robert not to waste so much money as he does on things that he could enjoy just as well in a museum, and which can never be made quite safe in a private house."

Rhoda stared at her stupidly.

If Lady Sarah's expressed opinion was not genuine, it was an excellent piece of acting. She was frank, sympathetic, kindly, and not in the least inclined to exaggerate the importance of the loss, or to impute blame to Rhoda.

"It's—it's a dreadful thing for me," stammered Rhoda, without quite knowing whether she was or was not ashamed of her own suspicions.

"Why? You surely don't suppose we think it was your fault? As Sir Robert himself says, it is just as likely that his keys were used as that yours were."

Rhoda shook her head.

"They were taken out of my pocket—and put back again," she said shortly. "They were missing when I first came back from the Priory, and they were restored during the time I was talking to Sir Robert about it."

"Then they were taken by some one who must have watched you go in and out of your room?"

"Yes."

"Does Sir Robert know that?"

"Not yet. I only found the keys replaced ten minutes before I came down to dinner."

"He will be in here within a few minutes now, and we will consult together about laying a trap for the thief."

Rhoda said nothing. She was confused, her head seemed to be spinning. There was no hint of any accusation in Lady Sarah's manner, nothing but sympathetic regret for the girl's own sake in her voice and manner.

But yet Rhoda did not trust her, did not even now really doubt that her first impression was the correct one. She looked at the fire, and turning suddenly, caught an expression in Lady Sarah's eyes which was not at all benevolent.

And she was completely reinstated in her first opinion. It was Lady Sarah, and no other, who, for what motive she did not yet know, had lain in wait for an opportunity of obtaining the keys, had obtained the possession of the three snuff-boxes, and who had then found means of replacing the keys in the pocket while she knew Rhoda to be downstairs.

"Well, it won't happen again," said Rhoda drily. "I am going to give back my keys to Sir Robert this evening, and I will never take charge of them again."

"He won't let you give them up."

"He will have no choice," said Rhoda, with decision.

"How obstinate you are," complained Lady Sarah petulantly.

"I don't think any one would act differently in my position," said Rhoda.

"Then he is to lose your help, after having learnt to depend upon it?"

Rhoda, with a flush in her cheeks, and speaking in a trembling voice, rushed nervously at the opportunity thus presented:

"Well, why don't you give him the help he wants yourself? It's easy enough, and think how grateful he would be to you! When he prizes every word and look from you, it would make him so happy if you only would interest yourself in his collection. Do this, take care of his keys yourself, and whatever you don't care to do, in the way of cataloguing and deciphering notes, and all that, give to me yourself, and let me do it for you instead of for him."

Rhoda spoke earnestly, almost passionately; and Lady Sarah, who had begun by laughing a little at her proposition, listened to the end of her speech with an unusually grave face.

There was a short pause when Rhoda had finished; then the volatile lady recovered her spirits.

"I wish I could," she said, with a pretty little shrug. "Believe me, I only wish I had been 'built that way,' and that I could play Joan to Sir Robert's Darby in the proper manner. But I really couldn't, you know. I might play at it for a week, but I couldn't keep it up. We don't like the same things, and it would be foolish of me to pretend to, because he'd find me out. Just think what a hash I should make of it if I were to attempt to criticise his Romney and his two Gainsboroughs, his Fra Angelico and his old engravings! To me they seem all dull and old-fashioned and over-rated altogether. I pretend sometimes to see their beauties, but it's only pretence, and it bores me to pretend. Don't you see?"

Rhoda was interested. If Lady Sarah had been acting before, she was obviously sincere now, and the girl felt for a moment rather sorry for the young married woman.

"Well, can't you teach him to be interested in the things that interest you?" she hazarded.

She was surprised at her own boldness; but there was something more human, less artificial than usual in Lady Sarah's manner that evening, which encouraged her to speak out. It was better to get right to the bottom of this human soul, if she could, now that she seemed to have the opportunity.

Lady Sarah shook her pretty head.

"Oh, dear no. When you lecture me——"

"Oh, no, I didn't!" interpolated Rhoda, shocked.

"Yes, you did. I repeat, when you lecture me, you do it without understanding the position. Every one is sorry for Sir Robert, the grave, kind-hearted man married to a flighty little woman who doesn't care about old masters or cracked teapots. But nobody takes the trouble to remember that there's another side to the question, and that the flighty little woman is to be pitied too!"

"Yes, I see," admitted Rhoda.

"It may be much more dignified, and a sign of a higher nature, and all that to prefer looking at pictures to dancing and motoring. But if one can't help oneself, what is one to do? And it would, of course, be just as impossible to make Sir Robert take to waltzing and to interest him in polo and fox-hunting, as it would to make a bookworm and a blue-stocking of a poor ignoramus like me."

Rhoda could not help smiling sympathetically. This was the truth for once. Lady Sarah was, for the moment at least, genuinely sorry for herself, and she made Rhoda sorry too.

"But you know what he was like in the first place," objected she timidly.

"Well, and he knew what I was like. And I can't suppose that he ever expected me to fall down and worship his Bartolozzis, or to go crazy over his old blue china. As for me, to do me justice, I never pretended that I could. So of what use would it be for me to try to do what isn't natural to me? Isn't it better that he should follow his bent, and I mine, when neither of us does anything wrong or mischievous, after all?"

"It seems a pity," ventured Rhoda. "Forgive me for saying so, but you wouldn't have to pretend much to be interested in what interests him."

"Yes, I should. Luckily, we have some pleasures in common. We like the same people. We have both taken a fancy to you, and we are both fond of his late ward, Jack. And we both adore Caryl. Why shouldn't we be content with the sympathies that we have, and not try to manufacture others?"

It was all very cleverly put, Rhoda thought, but she was not convinced. Perhaps Lady Sarah, frank as she seemed, did not expect her to be. At any rate, she suddenly sprang up from her stool, as if tired of the discussion, and flitting across to the piano, seated herself at it, and played a two-step with vigour that caused it to reach the ears of the gentlemen, whom it effectually brought out of the dining-room.

The talk at once turned again to the subject of the stolen snuff-boxes. Rhoda told Sir Robert of her discovery of the keys, was sure that they had been replaced in the pocket of her dress during her short absence to speak to him in the study, and insisted on returning them to him, declining to have the custody of them for the future.

It was in vain that the baronet protested, that Lady Sarah coaxed, that Jack said she should keep them and lay traps to catch the thief on a later occasion. Nothing would move her from her purpose, and Sir Robert had, with great reluctance, to accept the keys from her.

They all had theories to suggest, Jack being loud in support of the suggestion that the theft was the work of one of the men-servants, and Sir Robert being of opinion that it was the work of a woman. For, he said, no suspicion would be excited by the sight of one of the maids coming out of or going into a bedroom, while if a man-servant were to be caught in the neighbourhood of the rooms where he had no business, suspicion would be directed to him at once.

The conversation was animated, every one taking a fair share with the exception of Rhoda, whose attitude was rather that of a listener than of a talker.

And she was rewarded for her watchfulness by catching a look exchanged between Lady Sarah and Jack Rotherfield, a look after which her old suspicions returned in full force.

For in it she saw that there was a perfect understanding between these two over the theft, and that each seemed to be congratulating the other upon a lucky escape.

CHAPTER X.
THE STOLEN "ROMNEY"

IN spite of the strength of her suspicions, it was strange that Rhoda's interest in Lady Sarah grew stronger from that evening when she became fairly certain in her own mind that the lady had appropriated the snuff-boxes from her husband's collection.

Torn by doubts as to what the meaning of the theft could be, since Lady Sarah seemed to be plentifully supplied with money, on the one hand, and since she seemed to have no intention of getting Rhoda into disgrace, upon the other, Rhoda scarcely wavered in her belief.

She could not, certainly, have offered any very sound reasons for it; but with the illogical springing to an opinion which so often serves with a woman as well as strong reasoning powers, she caught and held fast to the idea that Lady Sarah had stolen the snuff-boxes, and moreover, that Jack Rotherfield knew all about it.

In spite of this belief, however, Rhoda felt that she had more sympathy with Sir Robert's erratic wife after that night than she had had before. The few moments' talk they had had together had opened her eyes to the fact that, if Sir Robert was disappointed in the woman who had inspired such a passion within him, she, on her side, was by nature unfitted to find much happiness or even contentment in his society.

Her husband bored her.

There was something in the mellow tones of his voice that irritated and depressed her, something in his sedate manner that seemed to her ridiculous when it was not deadening.

For while he had married her under the influence of passion, she, on her side, had been under the influence of no such idealising feeling.

On the one hand, he was the more to be pitied, in that he had married her under the spell of an illusion. On the other, she had been practically forced by circumstances to give her hand to a man who, whatever her respect for him might be, could not, in the nature of things, be expected to realise her girlish ideal.

Rhoda was very unhappy. No further allusion was made by Sir Robert to his loss, and she helped him as before. But they could not help feeling conscious of that unfortunate incident, and worrying their heads about it, while Lady Sarah was always making new suggestions as to traps and plots for the discovery of the dishonest person, to none of which the good-natured baronet would agree.

On the third day after the loss they all got something fresh to occupy themselves with, in the return home of Minnie Mallory and her brother George, who had got an extension of his vacation on the plea of ill-health:

he having had a slight attack of what he said was influenza, of which he had made the most.

They were much amused to hear who Rhoda was, having retained a dim remembrance of the tall pale girl with the lank hair who had told George that listening at keyholes was ungentlemanly.

They came up to her tumultuously, a couple of overgrown, sandy-haired, light-eyed, sharp-featured young people, with mischief in every line of their faces, and dry humour in every turn of their heads.

Rhoda was upstairs in Caryl's sitting-room when they presented themselves to her, grinning with pleasure.

"You don't remember me," said Rhoda.

"No," said George frankly. "I was only eight, and I don't think I should have recognised you with your hair up."

"Do you think we've altered very much?" demanded Minnie.

"Why, of course you have. You were only quite a little girl?"

"Do you think we've improved?" asked George.

"I hope so, I'm sure," said Rhoda frankly.

"That's not what I call civil," objected George.

"Oh, yes, it is. Because of course I shouldn't say it if I didn't feel sure you had improved very much," explained Rhoda.

"Why, what was wrong with us?" he asked brusquely.

"You used to listen at doors."

"Oh, so we should do now, if we got the chance," said Minnie calmly.

"I do like," said George, "to know what's going on all round me. Is Jack here still?"

Rhoda grew red.

"He has been here. He went away two days ago."

"Ah!" said George. "That's why Aunt Sarah is in such a bad temper."

"Hush," said Rhoda shocked.

"Why should I hush? Everybody knows that's true, except of course Uncle Robert. Aunt is always ill-tempered when she's left alone with him."

Rhoda kept frowning and looking at Caryl, in the endeavour to stop the rash young man. At last she got up, and beckoned to George to follow her to the window, while Minnie remained with the boy.

"You really mustn't talk like that about Lady Sarah, and especially before Caryl," she said.

"Oh, well, there's no harm in what I said. As for Aunt's ill-temper, the poor little beggar must have noticed it himself. And as for my speaking about her flirtation with Jack Rotherfield, everybody knows all about that. It's gone on for ever so long. That's why nobody notices it, except, of course, Minnie and me."

"I don't think you ought to talk like that. Sir Robert would be very angry if he were to hear you."

"No, he wouldn't. He wouldn't believe it, you know."

"I'm quite sure it would annoy him very much if he were to hear the way you talk."

"But he won't hear it. Bless your heart, do you think I don't know that it's only a safety-valve for Aunt?" said George with the air of an astute critic. "If it were not for Jack Rotherfield's visits, she'd sling her hook altogether."

"Oh, hush!"

"She would, I tell you. Even my grandmother knows it. That's why I call him a safety-valve."

Rhoda could scarcely believe her ears when she heard this young lad of twenty presuming thus to criticise his elders. The fact that there was at least a grain of truth in what he said made him, however, difficult to contradict, as he was impossible to silence.

"I should think," she said severely, "that your society and that of your sister was lively enough to keep Lady Sarah amused."

"Oh, no, she can't flirt with me, and it's flirtation she wants. It's like oil to the engine with her. I suppose it is with everybody."

"Not to Sir Robert," said Rhoda with dignity.

"Oh, yes, to him too. Doesn't he flirt with you?"

Rhoda was aghast at this impertinence.

George hastened to explain.

"In the nicest possible way, of course. But I should have thought he would have been delighted to get you to help him with his collection and things like that. You're so quiet and gentle, you would be just the sedative he requires after a dose of Aunt Sarah."

Rhoda was beyond measure shocked at this audacious speech, uttered as it was as if it had been the most natural and innocent in the world.

"I certainly never 'flirt,' as you call it, with Sir Robert, or with anybody," she said with dignity.

"Well, don't be angry. I didn't mean to say anything to annoy you. As I say, it's only natural to flirt with somebody, and I suppose my uncle makes confidantes of his Gainsborough ladies. Even a picture would be more sympathetic than my aunt when Jack's away."

Rhoda was greatly scandalised by this short conversation with The Terrors, whom she found still worthy of their name, as Mrs. Hawkes had predicted. She was, besides, rendered uneasy by the lad's perspicacity with regard not only to his aunt, but his uncle. The expression he had used, 'to flirt,' was odious and horrid. But there could be no doubt that in the main his contention, better expressed, would have been sound. Not only were the ill-mated pair happier apart than together, but each certainly found happiness in the society of others. Sir Robert looked the picture of content when he was hunting among his notes with Rhoda on one side of him and Caryl on the other; while Lady Sarah's low spirits disappeared as if by magic when Jack Rotherfield came into the room.

She wondered how this over-frank young man got on with his uncle and aunt, and had the satisfaction of seeing, at dinner-time, that The Terrors had tact enough to affect a guileless air of innocence in the presence of their guardians.

Only when it was perfectly safe to do so did George, after some allusion to Jack Rotherfield, glance over at his sister and bestow upon her a slight wink, which she promptly responded to in the same graceful fashion.

It was a childlike question put by Minnie to her aunt which elicited the reply that Jack Rotherfield would be again at Dourville in a week.

"I'm so sorry. I shall miss him," said George sweetly.

"Perhaps he won't miss you, dear," said his sister solemnly.

Luckily only Rhoda guessed at the veiled sarcasm in the ingenuous speech.

It was terrible to have to hear these two precocious young people sitting in judgment on their elders; they made her feel shy of entering the study to help Sir Robert, and she was aware that there was a grave interchange of glances between the two dreadful young people when the baronet made any remark about her work for him.

She was quite glad when George had to go back to Sandhurst, as, although she was aware that Minnie watched and noted as well in her brother's absence as if he had been there, still there was now no one with whom she could exchange her stealthy little looks, and that, Rhoda felt, was a relief.

When Jack came back in the following week, Lady Sarah seemed to wake up into life again, as The Terrors had said. Sir Robert, too, took as much pleasure as before in his society, and enjoyed it as guilelessly as ever.

It was on the second night after Jack Rotherfield's arrival at the Mill-house that Rhoda, who always slept with her window open and the curtains drawn back, woke up about one o'clock and fancied that she saw a moving light in the garden. At first not more than half awake, she watched the glimmer vaguely, without even wondering what it was. Then, her drowsiness suddenly yielding to complete wakefulness, she sat up in bed and looked out.

Yes. There certainly was an unusual light in the garden, and crossing the floor quickly, she saw that it was the reflection of some unseen light that she saw flickering on the grass by the side of the water.

At first she was rather alarmed, thinking that there might be a policeman with his lantern in the grounds, and that some one might have got in for an unlawful purpose.

There had been, at various times, small thefts discovered of plants and fruit from the grounds, which were extensive and in some parts easy of access from outside.

But then a fresh thought struck her. The wing containing the long gallery, which housed Sir Robert's collection, extended northwards to some distance from the main building, and was screened from her sight by shrubs and trees.

It now occurred to Rhoda that the light she saw might be reflected through the windows of the gallery, and the horrible fear flashed through her mind that the building might be on fire.

After watching for some moments, however, she decided that the light was too steady, and again it occurred to her to wonder whether any unauthorised person had got inside. Now that Sir Robert kept both sets of keys himself, she was free from responsibility, but her interest in the collection being as strong as ever, she could not rest until she had ascertained the meaning of the light.

Hastily dressing, with her eyes always keenly watching, she slipped out of her room and down the stairs.

Half way down she stopped, clammy and cold, with a sudden sickly recollection of the night, ten years before, when she had glided down the stairs in similar fashion.

For the moment memory rose up so strong within her, that she could almost have fancied she heard again the struggle going on in the drawing-room, and that she saw once more, in the moonlight, the blood-stained hand which she now knew to have been that of Jack Rotherfield.

The idea seized her that now she would find him involved in a fresh mystery, and recoiling from a possible discovery, she had turned, almost resolved to creep back to her room and give up her expedition, when the sound of a key turned in a lock struck her ear.

There was something going on, something wrong. For Sir Robert's sake she must conquer her repugnance, and find out what it was. She almost prayed that she might find that a burglar had got into the house, but she knew that the solution of the mystery would be something more unpleasant than that.

Hurriedly reaching the bottom of the staircase, she turned in the direction of the gallery. She had to pass through Sir Robert's study, and the door of this room she found suspiciously left open. So too was the door beyond, which led into the little passage at the end of which was the door leading into the gallery.

As she entered the study, and made her way across to the opposite door, she became aware of a tell-tale sound: it was a whisper. She could not hear any words: she could not distinguish the voice; but the fact was conclusive: since some one whispered, there must be some one to whisper to; there were at least two persons somewhere close by, and Rhoda had no difficulty in making a guess who those two persons were.

And, remembering the disappearance of the snuff-boxes, she could have little doubt as to the sort of errand which had taken them to Sir Robert's gallery.

Lady Sarah had robbed her husband before, she had now apparently taken an accomplice to help her to rob him again.

This was the thought in Rhoda's mind, as, full of indignation, and regardless of the consequences to herself, she crossed the floor of the study, and groped her way into the passage beyond.

There was no light there, and she presently hesitated, filled with the uncanny fear none of us can help in the dark, in the presence of some one whom we cannot see, but who, we have reason to think, may be able to see us.

For, compared with the pitchy blackness of the passage into which she was stepping, the study behind her was light.

She paused. Dead silence.

She took one step forward nervously.

There was a rush of air, and then she found herself seized, blindfolded, gagged, and lifted off her feet. She tried to cry out, but a hand was over her mouth. She felt herself flung down upon something which was not hard, and then stifled, suffocated, buried.

Again she tried to cry out, but the only result was that she felt herself thrust down, breathless, panting, gasping, fighting for air under a great and oppressive weight.

She struggled, but in vain, and then, half fainting, she lay quite still.

Then again she fancied that she heard a whisper, which seemed to come from a long way off. The weight was removed, there was a slight noise, and struggling once more, she suddenly found herself free, and safe, and alone.

Then she understood what had happened to her. She had been thrown on the springy morocco-covered couch in the study, covered over with all the available cushions, hassocks, and table-cloths, and then, when she ceased to struggle, she had been left to herself, with the result that her first movement had landed her on the floor, where she found herself surrounded by the tablecloths and cushions which had been used to stifle her cries.

She scrambled to her feet, groped her way to the door, and went through into the hall.

Whom should she rouse? Although she felt sure that the thieves would not be discovered, that the affair would end as the theft of the snuff-boxes had done, yet it was necessary for her own sake that she should make known at once the adventure she had passed through.

So she went upstairs to the housekeeper's bedroom, told her what had happened, and asked her to inform the baronet of her suspicions that some one had broken into the gallery.

Ten minutes later the whole household was astir. Mrs. Hawkes had roused Sir Robert, who gave directions that the menservants were to be sent into the grounds to look for the supposed burglar, and in the meantime he himself came out of his room, and learned all that Rhoda had to tell him on his way downstairs.

On reaching the gallery, and turning up the electric light, the baronet was not long in discovering the nature of the fresh loss he had sustained. The Romney, a beautiful picture of Lady Hamilton, had been cut neatly out of its frame.

The sky-light in the roof of the gallery was broken, and all hands, including those of Lady Sarah and Jack Rotherfield, who were among those roused by the commotion, pointed up to this, by which they all supposed that the burglars had made their entrance.

Amid the general commotion, however, a shrill girlish voice piped out:

"They didn't get in that way. Somebody broke the glass with that pole."

It was The Terror, Minnie Mallory, who made this announcement, pointing drily as she did so to the long pole, with a hook at the end, which was used to draw backwards and forwards the blind which kept out, when necessary, the strong sunlight.

The words caused a singular sensation in the assembled group. They were received at first in dead silence, and then there were whispers and stealthy glances exchanged.

Lady Sarah went up to her husband, and slid her hand confidentially through his arm:

"Send them away," she whispered. "I don't believe it's a burglar at all. Remember how the snuff-boxes went. Depend upon it, the picture's gone the same way."

"What way?" faltered Sir Robert, in a voice as low as her own.

"Better not ask," she whispered back.

Gradually, as it were melting away, the little crowd broke up, dispersed. There was a horrible sense of mystery and guilt upon everybody. The members of the household almost felt as if they individually had been concerned in the robbery of Sir Robert.

Rhoda found herself left alone, and as she went back to her room, sick at heart, with the whispers of the household buzzing in her ears, she remembered that Sir Robert had not addressed one word to her since making the discovery of the loss of his picture.

Was it possible that he suspected her?

What had Lady Sarah whispered to him?

Rhoda, with her sickening, deadly, knowledge of the truth, knowledge almost as certain as if she had seen the faces and heard the voices of the thieves, felt that her brain reeled under the weight of the secret she had to bear.

Suddenly she was startled, as she went slowly up the stairs, by feeling a small, thin hand tucked into her arm.

"Nice business this, isn't it?"

She started. It was Minnie Mallory who spoke, and in her light eyes Rhoda saw that she too made a shrewd guess at the truth.

"Hush!" said Rhoda.

"Oh, yes, it is 'Hush' this time—till George comes home," retorted Minnie as she nodded and left her to go to her own room.

Rhoda went back to hers in a sort of dream. She scarcely slept that night, and the next day she was pale, haggard, and miserable.

Nobody talked of anything but the robbery. Jack professed his intention of going to Scotland Yard and giving information to the police about the theft.

"Such a thing as a valuable picture," said he, "can easily be traced when the thieves offer it for sale."

Sir Robert seemed to acquiesce in this proposal, and soon after breakfast Jack Rotherfield's motor-car came round to take him up to town.

Rhoda was watching the packing of the luggage inside the car with curious eyes. Presently a gun-case was brought out of the house by a footman, who went indoors again when he had stowed it away.

With flushed cheeks and brilliant eyes Rhoda walked deliberately down the two broad stone steps, and took the gun-case out of the motor-car.

As she did so, she looked up, and her eyes met those of Jack Rotherfield, who was standing on the other side of the car.

"What are you doing?" said he. "That's my gun-case."

Rhoda, now as pale as a moment before she had been red, looked at him steadily.

"I'm going to take it into the study," said she. "I'm going to open it, in the presence of Sir Robert."

"The devil you are," retorted the young man, and a look of diabolical rage shot out of his dark eyes. "Give it back to me, Miss Pembury. You are behaving like a mad woman."

But Rhoda had turned, and, with the gun-case held fast, had run back into the house.

The next moment she, half-way to the study, found herself tapped sharply on the shoulder. Jack Rotherfield was behind her, stooping to whisper to her.

"What are your terms?" asked he in her ear.

"Take out what is inside this case, and leave it with me," said she in a voice as low as his.

"All right," said he sullenly.

The next moment, in the half-light of the passage, he had opened the gun-case, taken out something rolled up in brown paper, and thrust it angrily into her arms.

"There you are then. Confound you!" growled he, as he turned quickly away with the empty case.

Rhoda's brain reeled again.

She knew that she had got the Romney safe in her arms.

CHAPTER XI.
THE PICTURE RECOVERED

IN the half-dark passage Rhoda stood, alone, when Jack Rotherfield had left her, uncertain what to do.

The first impulse of thankfulness and delight, in the thought that she had rescued Sir Robert's favourite picture, that in a few moments he would be congratulating himself on its safe return, was quickly succeeded by a feeling of horror, of dread, when she realised the ever-increasing difficulties of her own position.

What should she say to him? How should she explain the manner in which she had obtained possession of the lost treasure?

To tell the whole truth was, for many reasons, out of the question.

In the first place, Jack Rotherfield, in asking her her terms, had, as it were, bound her in honour not to betray him; and, although she now appreciated the fact that, in keeping silence, she would be compounding a felony, she did not know what else to do.

Certainly Jack deserved to be denounced as a thief, and a traitor to his best friend. Remembering the horrible affair of ten years before, and that he had been concerned in it, she recognised that he must be a man wholly without conscience or sense of honour, since he could rob his best friend, deceive him, and even incur the guilt of a worse crime.

Whether the death of poor Langton were the result of murder or manslaughter, the silence of the man who had caused it gave reason for the worst suspicions.

But that was not by any means the whole of the difficulty. Even supposing that Rhoda had felt it her duty to denounce Jack to Sir Robert, regardless of the tacit obligation she was now under to be silent about his share in the theft of the picture, how could she take upon herself to open up such a disastrous series of questions as the baronet would naturally ask? How could she undertake the task of enlightening him as to the extent to which his own wife was involved in the deception which had been practised upon him?

And that it would be impossible to denounce Jack Rotherfield without involving Lady Sarah she felt sure.

Investigations would be made, interrogatories instituted, which would end in complete discovery. Even short of that, Rhoda doubted whether Lady Sarah would suffer her accomplice to be found guilty without confessing, tacitly or otherwise, to her share in his guilt.

But granted that even that difficulty were safely surmounted, and Jack Rotherfield ostracised, would not the result have consequences to be dreaded?

If Sir Robert were once to learn of the theft, he would certainly go on to learn the share Jack had had in the murder of the servant. And what questions would then be asked? What revelations would be made?

Again Lady Sarah's name would be introduced into the discussion, and the tottering fabric of the domestic happiness of both husband and wife would come down with a crash.

Precarious as it was, Rhoda knew that the position was better left alone: her aim must be to consolidate such domestic peace as was possible in the household, not to involve the family in irretrievable ruin.

Uncertain and miserable, she remained standing in the darkest part of the passage which led from the hall to the study, at one moment taking a step forward to the room where she knew Sir Robert to be, at another moving slowly in the opposite direction, with the idea of carrying the picture up to her own room until she should have prepared the way for its restoration.

What if she were to leave it at the study door, for Sir Robert to find when he should come out?

But she shrank from the thought of this. For might it not involve her in difficulties of her own? Might it not result, if she were to restore it thus in an underhand way and without a word of explanation, that she herself would be suspected to have had a hand, not only in the restoration of the picture, but in the theft of it?

She shuddered at the thought. Not for the world would she have risked the loss of the baronet's good opinion. She must find some better way than that of giving back the treasure.

She had not yet made up her mind, when she heard a light rustling on the stairs above her, saw the flutter of a lacy petticoat, caught a glimpse of a jewelled hand. Then, before she could move from where she stood, Rhoda found herself a prisoner. Lady Sarah was beside her, blocking the way to retreat.

"What's that?" asked she in a low voice, touching the parcel which the girl carried in her arms.

But Rhoda, in the half-darkness, only looked reproachfully into her face, without uttering a word. She was sure that Lady Sarah knew as well as she did what she was holding, and that she knew, too, what had happened. Indeed there was just enough of a certain acerbity underneath the lady's assumed frivolity of manner as she touched the roll, for Rhoda to be certain that Jack, before going, had told her everything.

Receiving no verbal answer, Lady Sarah looked up closely into the face of the other. Then she nestled up to her in the most caressing manner.

"You are ill," she said. "What is the matter? Come with me, come into my room and let me look at you. Yes, yes, I insist."

Rhoda would have resisted, protested, would have made her escape. But there was no getting away from the self-willed mistress of the house when she had made up her mind.

Lady Sarah had made no further inquiries about the parcel which Rhoda was holding tightly in her arms, and this reticence was suggestive.

"I'm not ill indeed. I'm going to my room," said Rhoda.

"No, no, you'll come to my boudoir first."

She led the girl up the stairs, and they entered the beautiful room with its silk panels and white enamel, and here Lady Sarah made Rhoda sit by the fire, and, taking a chair close to her, asked again, "Now, what is it? Tell me all about it. What's that you're carrying?"

Rhoda turned towards her with sudden fierceness.

"You know very well what it is," she said.

For a moment the spoilt beauty was taken aback. The colour faded out of her lips and cheeks as she sat back in silence. Rhoda looked at her steadily:

"You know what this parcel is, and you know how I got it," she went on.

Lady Sarah recovered herself.

"Really I don't understand you," she said coldly. "I haven't the least idea what it is you are carrying."

"Yes, you have, you know it's the picture, the Romney, which was stolen from the gallery. And more than that, you know who it was that stole it," cried Rhoda defiantly.

Lady Sarah drew a long breath. She was frightened, in spite of her *aplomb*, and for the moment she did not know how to meet this direct attack.

Rhoda burst into tears.

"Oh, Lady Sarah, what is the use of pretending? You know all about it, and as I know it too, what is the use of acting? It's a dreadful thing, a terrible thing, and it's very hard that I should be dragged into it, that I should have had to be obliged to do what I did to get it back. No, don't look as if you didn't know all about that too. Mr. Rotherfield told you, I'm sure, before he went away."

Lady Sarah was leaning on her hand. She was now deadly white, and her eyes seemed to have become twice their natural size. With laboured breathing she gasped out:

"What are you going to do? I don't admit anything. I don't know anything. But just tell me what you have in your mind."

"I must give the picture back to Sir Robert. And—I must tell him how I got it. There is no help for it, is there?"

74

Lady Sarah sprang off her chair and walked rapidly up and down the room, her draperies flying about her, her hair disordered, her face haggard with strong emotion. Then, quite unexpectedly, she paused in her walk, and then threw herself on her knees in front of Rhoda.

Clasping her hands together, she placed them on the knees of the other woman, and looked up earnestly into her face.

"Do you know what will happen, if you do that?" she asked abruptly.

Rhoda hesitated.

"You've got to know what you're doing," went on Lady Sarah. "Mind, I know nothing about this picture affair. I've heard nothing but what you've told me. But I gather that what you're carrying in that roll is the picture which was stolen out of the gallery last night."

"You know it is."

"I know nothing. But let us say that it is the picture. What are you going to tell Sir Robert?"

Rhoda hesitated again. Lady Sarah went on passionately:

"Are you going to make up some story of its having been restored to you?"

"I'm going to tell the truth," cut in Rhoda brusquely. "I'm going to say that I watched the packing of Mr. Rotherfield's luggage inside his car, that I saw the gun-case put in, that I took it out with my own hands, and that Mr. Rotherfield followed me back into the house, stopped me, and let me take the picture out."

"How did you know—supposing this strange story is true—that the picture was in the gun-case?"

"I guessed it."

Lady Sarah looked alarmed.

"You are very inquisitive," she said sharply.

"Oh, Lady Sarah, how can I help it, when such things happen as have happened here?"

Lady Sarah drew a deep breath.

"Things! What things?" escaped her lips in spite of herself.

"Well, I know more than I have told you. Not through any curiosity on my part, but because I couldn't help it."

Lady Sarah looked askance at her, but did not venture to ask any more questions.

"Go on," she said petulantly. "Go on with this fairy tale that you intend to tell Sir Robert."

"That's all. It will be for Sir Robert himself to make inquiries. All I have to tell him is how I became possessed of the picture."

"Very well," said Lady Sarah, in an attitude and with an expression of calm despair. "And do you know what will happen when you've told him?"

"It will not concern me. I shall have done what I had to do, and I shall go away."

"After having succeeded in wrecking Sir Robert's happiness and mine. Oh, yes, it is of no use to shake your head, that is what you will have done. Do you think he will be content to receive back the picture, and to accept your story, without making any inquiries? It is absurd to think such a thing. He will certainly find out that you have not told him the truth, because he knows Jack, and can trust him, and Jack will assure him that there is no truth in your preposterous story. But you will have sown the seed of mistrust in my husband, and you will have spoilt every chance there was of our continuing to live happily together. And that after your lectures to me, after your assurance that you were so grateful to him that all you wished for was his happiness!"

Rhoda was crying quietly, with her face hidden. She knew that the picture drawn by Lady Sarah would probably prove to be, in its main outlines, correct. Jack and Lady Sarah would certainly deny all that Rhoda said, and it was scarcely likely that, in the long run, with his admiration for his wife and his fondness for Jack at war with his confidence in Rhoda, he would end by taking her part against the other two.

Nevertheless, even if he allowed Rhoda to go away in disgrace, perhaps herself under suspicion of having committed the theft, it was probable that, as Lady Sarah suggested, the seeds of mistrust would have been sown within him, and there would be a change for the worse in the domestic life of the household.

Suddenly Rhoda looked up, in desperation.

"What can I do?" she asked. "I can't let him be deceived. And Mr. Rotherfield is behaving infamously, Lady Sarah; he is robbing his best friend. Don't deny it. You know that it is the truth; at least, that it is part of the truth."

Lady Sarah turned pale again.

Then she suddenly unclasped her hands, and clung to Rhoda, coaxing, piteous, irresistible. It was part of the charm of this wayward woman that she could transform herself, without a moment's notice, into a sort of grown-up child, helpless, weak, plaintive, lost in doubts and fears, begging for help, for kindness, for guidance.

That was what she seemed to be now, as she looked with imploring eyes into Rhoda's face, and whispered:

"Don't do it, don't do it, dear. You wouldn't like to break up the home, you wouldn't like to make poor Sir Robert miserable. Even if what you thought were true, that is what would happen, if you were to tell him what you mean to tell."

Rhoda trembled. It was almost impossible to resist the clinging hands, the appealing eyes, knowing as she did know that the danger of a break-up was real. Whatever might be the exact result of her telling Sir Robert the truth, as far as she knew it, Rhoda thought it more likely than not that it would take some tragic form.

"What do you suggest yourself that I should do?" she asked.

Lady Sarah recovered some of her brightness of manner, her alertness, upon the instant.

"I propose that you should give the picture to me, and that I should give it back to Sir Robert myself, telling him that the thief left it at the house, with a note begging to be forgiven for what he had done."

But Rhoda frowned impatiently.

"No, no," she said. "Don't tell him more lies. You may give back the picture yourself, if you like, but on condition that you tell the truth, that you confess who it was that stole it, and say that he, Mr. Rotherfield, has given it back and begs forgiveness. It will be a shock to him, of course, to find who it was that did it, but at any rate it is better that he should be shocked than that he should be further deceived."

Lady Sarah, however, shook her head.

"He would never forgive him. I couldn't tell him that. Unless," her face brightened, as a fresh idea struck her, "I might perhaps be able to persuade him that it was a rough practical joke! I might take the blame of that upon myself."

"Yes, yes. Sir Robert would forgive you anything, anything," urged Rhoda.

Already Lady Sarah had sprung up from her knees and seized the rolled-up picture.

"I'll go at once," said she, "and make him happy."

But Rhoda was not satisfied. Misgivings had seized her the moment she saw the lady's quick recovery from her depression. She was troubled, also, as to the extent to which she could rely upon her keeping her word.

"Lady Sarah," she urged in a trembling voice, "remember this is not the only thing that has to be given back. The snuff-boxes——"

But the spoilt beauty was already at the door. Looking back over her shoulder, and laughing mischievously, she said, quite in her old, buoyant, happy manner:

"Snuff-boxes! Oh, dear, I know nothing about those! If he suspects, he'll have to make his own discoveries. One surprise is enough for him at a time!"

And the next moment she had flitted out of the room, lightly tripping along, relieved from all care herself, but leaving Rhoda oppressed by a strong sense that she had not made the most of her opportunity.

She felt that she ought to have been more exacting, that she should have made more stringent conditions, that she ought perhaps even to have gone the length of insisting that she should accompany Lady Sarah on her errand to Sir Robert.

But it was too late for regrets, too late for anything but unwilling acquiescence in the bold plan which the wilful lady had conceived, for giving up the stolen Romney.

But Rhoda wondered, as she slowly went out of the boudoir, and to Caryl's room, where the boy was waiting for her, what story it was that Lady Sarah would end by telling her husband? Would she go as near the truth as she had promised to do? Would she confess to having been one of the conspirators, and to Jack Rotherfield's having been the other? And would she say, as she proposed, that the whole affair was nothing more than a practical joke?

If she did, would not even the gentle, unsuspicious Sir Robert turn round upon her with a question about the stolen snuff-boxes?

By no stretch of imagination could he be induced to believe, if once he were told that Lady Sarah and Jack were engaged in the robbery of the picture, that they were innocent of the other theft.

More and more slowly Rhoda walked, as she told herself, with a little shudder, that she could not trust Lady Sarah, and that the story she was telling her husband, whatever it be, would not implicate either herself or Jack Rotherfield.

CHAPTER XII.

LADY SARAH'S DUPLICITY

IF Rhoda could have followed Lady Sarah into the study, she would have discovered that her suspicions and forebodings were amply justified.

Sir Robert was deep in his studies when she entered like a whirlwind, with bright eyes and voluble tongue, bearing in her arms a roll in which the baronet altogether failed to recognise his lost picture.

"Bertie, Bertie, look here, I've news, good news for you!" she cried with excitement, as she dashed across the floor and plunged her burden into the midst of his letters and papers, his books and his writing materials.

"Good gracious, my dear, what is it?"

She sprang up, clapped her hands, nodded her head, and beamed upon him.

"See for yourself," said she.

He rose from his chair with a troubled look on his face. Although he now guessed what the surprise was which was in store for him, and although he had spent the night and morning in lamenting his loss, instinct told him that there was something to learn which he would rather not have known, in connection with the recovery of his treasure.

"What is it?" he asked hoarsely, as he touched the roll, and looked at her.

"I believe you know what it is," replied she, "but if not, I'll show you."

Her hands were wet and trembling, for all her affectation of gaiety and unconcern, and it was with difficulty she performed the simple task of tearing the paper from the roll, and exhibiting its contents to her husband.

"There!" she said, rather tremulously, as she unrolled it, "Your picture! Back again, and quite safe and unharmed, I believe."

But he looked at her with a frown.

"What does it mean?" he said hoarsely. "Who brought it back? Where does it come from?"

She glanced at him quickly. He was staring at the roll with a look of intense distress in his grave eyes. She drew her breath quickly, and glanced at him once more anxiously as she laughed, and said:

"I wish you would just take your luck, Bertie, without asking any questions."

"How can I? I must know."

"You'll be sorry, and—and you'll be angry," faltered she, her colour coming and going.

"Never mind. I think you can trust me to be just."

She suddenly made a spring at him, and held his arms, looking up with a bewitching air of entreaty into his face.

"Suppose some one you knew, and liked, and trusted, should have fallen a victim to a temptation too strong, under pressure of friends who wanted help badly. What then?"

"Well, who is it?"

His voice was stern, almost hard. Lady Sarah, frightened, began to weep.

"I can't tell you," she said quickly, "while you look like that. I daren't."

He patted her shoulder kindly.

"Nonsense," he said. "You can trust me to be just."

"I don't ask you to be just, I want you to be merciful. I want you to promise that you will accept this act of restitution without any questions, and that you will be satisfied not to speak of the matter again. The thief has repented, as you see, and has proved repentance."

"I must know who it is," said Sir Robert, with more sternness than he had ever used to his wife before.

"Yes, if you will promise to forgive and—forget."

"I promise," said Sir Robert after a pause.

He was looking pale and anxious in his turn, as he sat down, after placing a chair for his wife, and folding his hands, kept his head bent, as he waited for her promised revelation.

"What would you say if you were to learn that it was a lady in your employment, one who has proved herself very useful, very devoted, who yielded to a temptation she couldn't resist?" said she.

Sir Robert looked up sharply.

"I should say," said he quietly, "that it wasn't true."

Lady Sarah bit her lip, disconcerted.

"I swear to you," said she earnestly, after a short pause, "that it was she who gave me back the picture and begged me to give it to you and to ask you to say nothing, to ask nothing, but to be content to have recovered it."

He turned round to face his wife.

"Ask her to come and speak to me," said he quickly.

"If I do, she will leave the house at once. She told me so," said she sharply.

Sir Robert rose from his chair, and paced up and down the room.

"There is something more in this," said he with decision.

"Do you doubt my word?"

"Not for a moment, of course. But what I mean is that what she has told you is not the whole of the truth. She is shielding some one else, the guilty person."

Lady Sarah drew herself up.

"What is the divinity that hedges Miss Pembury," she asked haughtily, "that she must be considered incapable of any sort of error?"

80

He stopped and answered her steadily.

"She is a perfectly noble and irreproachable lady," he said, "and as incapable of a mean and despicable theft as you are yourself."

His wife looked down, with the blood rising in her cheeks.

"You will then be satisfied with her message. You won't try to find out anything more?" she said in a low voice.

"I will say nothing to any one at present," he said quietly. "I think, Sarah, you must be satisfied with that."

She looked at him doubtfully, but affected to think that he had given her the promise she wanted; and then she kissed him and tripped out of the room.

But she left her husband in a state of acute distress. It was not possible for him to believe that his wife had deliberately deceived him, although even that sometimes seemed more likely than that the patient, high-minded Rhoda should have been guilty of deception and ingratitude.

But he felt sure that he had only heard part of the story, and the conclusion to which he still clung, after turning the matter over in his mind, was that Rhoda was shielding some one else. Who that some one was, however, he had no idea. And that it could be the man who had been dear to him for so many years, in conjunction with his own wife, who had robbed him, never for one moment entered the baronet's mind.

He was far too loyal himself to suspect disloyalty in his nearest and dearest, and his conjecture was that it was some member of his household, one of the under servants, and not one of those who had been in his service many years, who had committed the theft both of the picture and of the snuff-boxes.

Knowing, as he did, that Rhoda had been the first to discover the theft of the picture, he decided that she must have found out more than she confessed to have done, but that she held her peace until she had forced the thief to restore at least part of the plunder.

Withal he was hurt to think that she had not come straight to him herself. Surely she might have known that she could come to him without fear, and that he would temper justice with mercy.

The consequence of this slight feeling of injury was a certain coldness in his manner when he met her at luncheon; and the unhappy Rhoda at once jumped to the conclusion that he suspected her of the theft. She thus did less than justice to him, and more than justice to his wife. For she little thought that the artful Lady Sarah had done her very best to divert suspicion from herself and Jack Rotherfield by accusing the companion of her little son.

Rhoda was heartbroken. She was crying quietly by herself in a distant corner of the grounds, when she suddenly found two long lean arms put round her neck from behind, and heard Minnie Mallory's voice in her ear, saying in tones of encouragement:

"Look here, don't you cry. Aunt Sally's been making mischief, I suppose, with Uncle Bertie?"

Rhoda was startled, and turning quickly, asked the girl what she meant.

By this time Minnie, with a battered and bent hat cocked over one eye, was squatting on the grass like a large-sized toad, looking up at her keenly out of her light eyes.

"What was in that gun-case?" she asked suddenly.

Rhoda dashed away her own tears and stared at the girl in dismay. Was Minnie a witch?

"W—w—what gun-case?" stammered she.

Minnie gave her a supercilious glance and a shrug.

"Oh, you know," she said. "That gun-case you took out of Jack's car just before he went away."

"A gun, I suppose," Rhoda replied quickly.

"Then what did you take it indoors for?"

There was a pause. Minnie shrugged her shoulders again.

"Oh, of course, you needn't tell me unless you like, but I can't help guessing, can I? And I can't help wondering why Jack looked so awfully cross when he came out again."

"You see quite enough, without being told anything," was Rhoda's comment.

Minnie nodded.

"Well, I do keep my eyes open, especially in a house like this, where there is so much to see. But I shouldn't cry, if I were you. Because nobody will ever blame *you* for anything that ever happens here."

There was a weird air of prophecy about this remark which made Rhoda feel uncomfortable. But she only sighed, and said:

"Nothing that happens will matter to me, for I am going away."

"Oh, no, you're not," croaked the witch.

"You'll see," said Rhoda, as she rose with an air of determination, and started to walk back to the house.

The mocking laughter of Minnie sounded uncannily in her ears, as she disappeared into the yew path.

She went straight to the study and knocked at the door. Almost at the same moment she became aware that some one was talking inside the room, and she would fain have retired. But as Sir Robert called out "Come in," she had to enter, blushing and apologetic, and then she found that Jack Rotherfield and Lady Sarah were both in the room with the baronet.

"I'm so sorry, I thought you were alone," said Rhoda.

"And he will be alone in a moment," cried Lady Sarah merrily. "Jack's had a breakdown, and he had to come back, and he's been telling us all about it."

It flashed through Rhoda's mind that, as Jack's errand to town had probably been connected with the disposal of the Romney, the breakdown had not been a very serious nor a very inconvenient one. And then, rendered suspicious by circumstances, she noted that Lady Sarah, in spite of her statement that she was going, did not go. And it occurred to Rhoda that Lady Sarah wished to avoid the possibility of a *tête-à-tête* between her husband and Rhoda.

Sir Robert turned to the girl courteously, and asked what he could do for her. In a low voice, striving to repress every sign of emotion, Rhoda said that she would be glad if she might leave the Mill-house at once, and return home to her parents.

The baronet did not seem surprised.

"Of course we can't keep you against your will," he said. "But I am very sorry, and we shall miss you very much. Have you spoken to Lady Sarah about it?"

She saw that he too was striving to speak more calmly than he felt.

"No. I thought I ought to come to you first."

"I can only repeat that I am more sorry than can say. And as for Caryl——"

He broke off, deeply moved. There was a pause, during which Rhoda noticed that though Lady Sarah appeared to be chattering idly to Jack she was watching with the keenest attention what went on between her husband and Caryl's companion.

"Thank you," said Rhoda. "I will say good-bye to Caryl at once, if I may."

"You are going to-day, then? It's rather sudden? For your own sake, if I might suggest, I should say you had better wait till to-morrow. You look tired, and unfit for a journey."

She raised her eyes to his face and gave him one swift glance. There was a world of feeling in her own sensitive face as she looked at him: gratitude, regret, affection, and even reproach, all expressed themselves in that one quick up-look of her tender blue eyes.

And the answering look which Sir Robert threw at her was hardly less eloquent. There was in his grave face a look of earnest affection, and an expression of almost childlike helplessness in the face of an unexpected blow.

Rhoda choked down a sob, and crossed the room quickly to Lady Sarah.

"I'm going away," she said quickly; and without thinking it necessary to give any explanation to a lady who, she was sure, must understand her decision without it, she added: "I'm going upstairs to say good-bye to little Caryl."

With Lady Sarah's perfunctory regrets ringing in her ears, mingled with the polite expressions of surprise from Jack Rotherfield, she went out of the room.

She crept up the stairs with her heart beating very fast. If it was hard to leave Sir Robert, what would the parting with poor little Caryl be?

He was lying by the window of his sitting-room, which had once been the nursery, and he clapped his hands as she came in.

"Oh, Rhoda, Rhoda, what a long time you've been! I'd thought you had forgotten me!" he cried, as soon as he caught sight of her.

And as she looked at his thin face, and saw the flush of pleasure in his cheeks and the brightness which came into his eyes, as the nurse got up, and, smiling, gave her chair to the new-comer, Rhoda felt as if her heart would burst.

"My dear Caryl," she said as she bent to kiss him, "I'm afraid you won't like to hear something I've got to tell you."

A look of vivid intelligence appeared on his face, and he glanced anxiously towards the nurse.

"Oh, is it what she says?" he asked tremulously. "Are you going away?"

Rhoda turned quickly. Had the possibility of her going been discussed, then, in the servants' hall?

"Yes, I've been here such a long time that my father and mother want to see me," she said, trying to speak brightly. "You wouldn't begrudge them a sight of their own daughter, would you?"

"Not just a look at them, I wouldn't begrudge you that," he said. And then he called, "Nurse!"

The girl came back into the room.

"What is it, Master Caryl?"

"Ask my father to come and see me, please."

Rhoda bent quickly to kiss him again, but he detained her, clinging to her.

"You must wait, you must wait a minute," he said feverishly.

And the touch of his hot hands made her shiver.

"If you want me to say good-bye to Sir Robert and Lady Sarah, I have just done so," said she.

But Caryl would say nothing about that.

"Sit down," he said, "and tell me what you've been doing, and where you've been. You've never left me so long alone before."

"Well, I've been in the grounds, Caryl."

"Yes, I saw you go. And I thought it very unkind of you not to take me. But I know why you didn't," and he pressed her hand with his little thin fingers. "You wanted to cry, that's why you wanted to be by yourself. And that's why you want to go home. You're not happy, Rhoda. You look so different from what you did at first, before mama came back."

"It's nothing to do with mama, Caryl," said Rhoda quickly.

"Oh no. But you have been crying, though?"

"Perhaps I have. Perhaps I don't like leaving you, Caryl."

He sighed, and played with her fingers quietly, and said very little more till his father came into the room.

Sir Robert looked flushed and uneasy; he caught sight of Rhoda at once; and the presence of the lady seemed to make him graver than ever.

"Come here, papa."

The baronet came and bent over his little couch.

"Give me your hand," said the boy.

The baronet obeyed, still without looking at Rhoda, who was trying to withdraw her fingers from the tight clutch of the child.

"Papa," said Caryl, "I sent for you because I want you to tell Rhoda not to go away and leave me."

Sir Robert gazed down at his little son.

"When a lady makes up her mind to do a thing, Caryl, it's not kind or courteous to try to dissuade her," said he.

But Caryl persisted.

"I don't believe she really wants to go, papa. I think she'll stay if you ask her to," said he.

"No, no, Caryl, I must go," said Rhoda hoarsely.

Sir Robert looked up then, and his eyes met hers. In his there was a look of grave, tender kindness of gentle reproach, which cut her to the heart.

"I never thought, Caryl, that she could have left you," he said in a low voice.

And Rhoda, bending suddenly very low over the child, hid her face and whispered:

"Caryl, you're don't know what you're asking, dear, but—I'll stay."

CHAPTER XIII.
SIR ROBERT SEEKS ADVICE

SIR ROBERT was watching the pair curiously: noting the feverish gladness with which the boy clung to Rhoda's hand, and the tenderness with which she, in return, bent over him.

It cost him a sharp pang to think that this was just the sort of way in which he should have liked his wife to bend over their invalid son. There was a motherly kindness in Rhoda's every look and touch, as she smoothed the boy's pillow or smiled at him, that realised completely Sir Robert's ideal of what a mother ought to be to her child.

Yet it was a stranger in blood who filled this office to the boy, and the visits of Caryl's mother were hasty affairs, undertaken in the intervals of the serious business of life, motoring, tennis-playing, dancing, travelling.

It was impossible that a bitter thought should not come into his mind at the sight.

Caryl turned his head, with a smile, to his father.

"I thought it would be all right, papa," said he, "when you came."

Rhoda could scarcely suppress a sob. She knew something of what was passing in Sir Robert's mind, for he had often uttered words expressive of his regret that Lady Sarah was not more domestic in her tastes. That that aspiration chiefly concerned the delicate boy it was not difficult to understand.

But now that the matter was settled, that Rhoda had promised to remain at the Mill-house, there was another question to be answered. Why had she been so anxious to go away? What, too, did she mean by these words, uttered half-unconsciously, as it seemed, to the boy: "You don't know what you're asking!"

Sir Robert had supposed, naturally enough, when Rhoda told him that afternoon that she wished to leave the house, that it was the unpleasant affair of the lost picture which had caused her so suddenly to make up her mind to leave a house where she had been subjected to such an alarming experience as that of the previous night. To a nervous woman, the night alarm, followed by a mysterious and not yet explained sequel, must have been quite sufficient to make her disinclined to stay in a house where such things had happened.

Now, however, on overhearing these whispered words to Caryl, which implied that she had something still to fear, Sir Robert was moved to strong curiosity.

He looked at her intently, and Rhoda blushed under his scrutiny.

Meanwhile Caryl, delighted to have carried his point, was playing affectionately with her right hand, and pressing it against his cheek.

Sir Robert was anxious to have an opportunity of putting some questions to Rhoda, and, with that idea in his mind, he smiled down at his little son and said:

"And now you've persuaded her to stay with you, Caryl, you mustn't be greedy, and expect to have her all to yourself. You must let mama see a little of her too, and me."

The boy looked up, smiling.

"I want her the most," said he. "You've got your pictures, papa, and mama's got Jack."

The words came quite naturally from the child's mouth, but they produced a most curious and painful impression upon his two hearers. Sir Robert seemed for the moment stunned by them, as, glancing at Rhoda, he saw upon her face an expression of dismay which was like a sudden illumination to him.

"Yes, we've got Jack too, of course," he said presently, recovering himself although there was a change in his voice, "but he isn't here always."

"Nearly always, when mama's here," persisted the boy simply. "And you've always got your pictures, haven't you? Anne says you've got back the one you thought was stolen."

Again there was a look upon Rhoda's face which roused Sir Robert's keenest attention and interest.

"Yes, I've got my picture back," said he. "Who told you about that?"

"Oh, I heard Anne talking about it to Mrs. Hawkes. That was this morning. And then when Anne came in a little while ago she told me you had got it back, nobody knew how."

Rhoda turned her head away, feeling that there was a guilty look on her face which Sir Robert's unusually penetrating gaze seemed to challenge. She did not want to meet his eyes again; ever since those first words of the boy's about Jack she had been conscious of an excitement, a restlessness in Sir Robert's demeanour, which were quite unusual with him, and she dreaded the thought of a *tête-à-tête* with him—which, however, she saw to be inevitable.

"By the bye, Miss Pembury, I should like to hear your account of the return of the picture," said the baronet in the gentlest of voices, as Rhoda took the opportunity, when father and son were looking at each other, to leave her post by the side of the couch, and to glide hastily towards the door.

He had followed her and was holding the door open for her.

"Are you going to take Rhoda away, papa?" piped out the small voice from the couch near the window.

"Not for very long. I'll ring the bell for Anne to come back to you for half an hour," said Sir Robert.

But the boy pouted.

"I don't want Anne," said he. "I can wait here by myself till Rhoda comes back. Don't be long, don't let papa keep you long," he cried, waving his thin hand as she went out.

Rhoda smiled back at him, with a trembling lip. She would have given the world to avoid the interview which the baronet was determined to force upon her. There was a gravity in his look quite different from the calm serenity of his everyday expression; she knew that an ugly thought concerning his wife and Jack Rotherfield had been obtruded upon his mind for the first time.

Was it better that he should know the danger? Perhaps so. But in any case it was a terrible thing for the girl that she had unconsciously helped to bring it home to his mind. The boy's innocent words might perhaps have passed unheeded, but for the point she herself had all unconsciously and unwillingly given them by her startled look.

And then, following that moment of revelation, there had come the speech about the picture, and again she thought that her face might perhaps have revealed some guilty knowledge concerning it.

They went slowly downstairs, Rhoda first, Sir Robert following in silence. It was not until they reached the hall that Sir Robert, taking a hat from the hall table, turned to her and said:

"Shall we take a turn round the garden? I want to speak to you."

There was no help for it. She bowed her head, and they passed out quickly by the garden-door, for she understood that his intention was to avoid Lady Sarah and possible interruptions, to which they might have been liable if they had gone straight to the study.

He led the way quickly to the water, crossed the rustic bridge, and so reached a beautiful grass path which could not be seen from the house.

Here he slackened his steps, and then he said in a very gentle tone:

"Please don't look so frightened, my dear Miss Pembury. I am not going to ask any awkward questions, believe me. I may say at once that I know you are shielding some one who was concerned in the disappearance of my picture, but I am not going to press you for any details which you may not feel inclined to give me. But I have had a rude shock within the last half-hour, following on an anxious time in connection with the disappearance of first the snuff-boxes and then the 'Lady Hamilton.' And I am obliged to come to you for—for advice, and—for guidance."

"I'm afraid I'm too stupid to be able to advise any one," said Rhoda timidly.

He made a gesture of denial.

"No, no. I quite understand the difficulty you are in, and I hope I shall not have to say anything to pain you. It is very hard on such a young woman as you are to find herself in such a position as that you are in. But you will help me if you can, I'm sure."

"Of course I would help you in any way I could. You won't press me to betray any secrets, I'm sure."

He looked at her quickly.

"Tell me," he said quite sharply, "whether, as far as you can see, I am neglecting any part of my duty to—to any member of my—my family."

Rhoda drew a long breath, and then suddenly found courage. Turning her blue eyes full upon him, she said, while the colour deepened in her cheeks and her lips quivered:

"Yes, Sir Robert, I think you are."

Although he had invited her to be candid, this speech evidently took him by surprise. He stared at her apprehensively, and then said with the utmost meekness:

"Will you tell me—to whom?"

"I think," stammered the girl, her breath coming fast, "that you are neglecting your duty to your wife."

This was direct indeed. He stopped short, made her stop too, and faced her roundly:

"How?" said he.

Rhoda knew that she must go on now, and she poured out all that was in her heart, without more ado.

"I think," she said, throwing out her words in little groups, with a strange, staccato stop after every few syllables, "that you ought to be with her more, not to let her go away without you, not to let her choose her own companions and friends. I think you ought to insist upon being her companion, her friend, yourself. Of course I know how hard it would be—that you don't care for the same things or the same places. But since she won't bend and give way, and do as she ought, I think you ought to do it all for her. You ought not to yield to her every caprice, to let her indulge every whim. If you go on running down one path while she is running down one that isn't even parallel with yours, how can it end but in your finding yourselves some day, so far apart that—that you can never come together again?"

It was plain speaking with a vengeance, and Rhoda would never have ventured upon it in cold blood. But when she was thus unexpectedly challenged by Sir Robert, she felt, honouring, respecting, loving him as she did, that there was nothing for her but to be daring, audacious, wholly, flagrantly honest, and to fling down thus before him her own views, without hesitation, without pause, and then, if necessary, ask for pardon.

But there was no need for that. In Sir Robert's face, as he listened to her, with head averted, tightly pressed lips, and eyes that seemed at last to open to look out upon the world around him as it was, and not as it ought to have been, there was a look which showed Rhoda that, however painful her words might be to utter and to hear, she had done right in speaking them.

Like a succession of blows her sentences fell upon him, each helping to drive home to him the truth which he, good, kind-hearted, amiable man that he was, had so long been in danger of ignoring.

He knew that there was no word of exaggeration in what she said, he was conscious that she was, on the whole, merciful to him. But her indictment was a severe one nevertheless, and at first he reeled under it.

There was a long pause, during which poor Rhoda, recovering from the impulse of passion which had urged her on, became more and more timid and apologetic, until the light faded out of her eyes and the tears welled up to them.

He, meanwhile, said nothing, but looked away to the hills, with the setting sun behind them, and stood so still that she wondered whether she had stunned him by her onslaught.

A sob escaped her, and then he turned slowly.

"That it should be left to you, a girl, to teach me my duty!" he said most gently. "I'm ashamed of myself, as I ought to be. Pray Heaven I haven't left it too late. Don't cry, child, don't speak until you've heard what I think. It's just this: it's a thousand pities I didn't know you as well as I do now half a dozen years ago. True, you were very young then, but I dare say you had ten times more sense, even then, in your head, than I have in mine now. Dry your eyes, child, dry your eyes," he went on in a brighter and more energetic tone: "You've got more to tell me, more help to give. Tell me, what you would advise? If it isn't too late how shall I begin?"

Her timidity, her hesitation were gone again in a moment. Rhoda was so desperately interested in him and his happiness that, as soon as an opening came for her to help, her instinct came to her aid and once more she said the right thing in the right way.

"Take her away," said she. "Don't let her go away by herself, but make her travel with you. When you're once away from your pictures and curios you will have to depend upon her. And you must teach her to depend upon you."

The advice was so shrewd, so good, that he looked at her for a few moments in silent admiration before he said:

"It's excellent advice, but do you think I can take it? Where should we go? I should be lost——".

"Ah!" cried Rhoda, putting up her finger warningly. "You mustn't be. That will be the hard part of it for you; in fact all the hardship will be yours. But you will have to take it, for she won't help you."

He nodded in meek but vague acquiescence.

"And where am I to take her?" he asked submissively.

"Why not to Egypt for the winter?" said Rhoda boldly. "You will find plenty to interest you there." And already she saw a light of interest in his eyes, "and the very novelty of the thing will be enough to please Lady Sarah."

He nodded appreciatively.

"It's a good suggestion certainly. But there will be difficulties."

"Plenty of them," admitted Rhoda. "But nothing that you won't be able to get over, now that you see there is danger in leaving her too much to herself and her own ways."

"Yes, yes. And Caryl——"

"You can trust him with me, can't you?"

The look of straightforward gratitude and trust on his face as he exchanged looks with her was balm to her heart.

"And now," he said, "I can't thank you. I can only pray that—that your advice has come—in time."

The look of gravity on his face showed Rhoda, who shivered as she glanced at him, that he appreciated the extent of the danger to which his easy-going temper had brought him and his wife.

Rhoda dared not say any more; she was in terror now lest he should proceed to question her about the picture and its restoration. But the baronet's whole attention was absorbed by the peril to his wife, and he had forgotten everything else in the one theme.

So Rhoda was able to make her escape to the house, where she was met on the stairs by Minnie, mocking, triumphant, stretching two long, thin arms across to bar her passage.

"I told you you would have to stay, didn't I?" asked she.

Rhoda felt almost shocked at the girl's uncanny perspicacity.

"Oh, yes, yes, it wasn't so difficult to predict that," she said, as she dived under one of Minnie's arms, and fled upstairs.

It was not until dinner-time that Rhoda met Lady Sarah or Sir Robert again; and she perceived, at the first glance, at Lady Sarah and Jack that they were both on thorns as to what had happened during the afternoon. They looked apprehensively from her to Sir Robert and back again, as if knowing that there was something interesting for them to hear.

Lady Sarah was most caressing and sweet to her husband, who received her advances with his usual gentleness, but not without a certain extra solemnity of manner which prepared her in some measure for what was to come.

It was not until dessert was reached, and the servants had left the room, that Sir Robert, glancing at his wife, and smiling in a manner which was not quite spontaneous, said:

"My dear, I've been preparing a little surprise for you, and I should like to know whether you will think it a pleasant one or not. Instead of your going to the Riviera this winter with your aunt and cousins I am going to take you to Egypt with me."

"With you! You're going to travel!" gasped Lady Sarah, quite openly dismayed by the prospect.

A cloud appeared on her husband's brow.

"Yes," said he. "I've never been there myself, and I think I should enjoy it as much as you would. I hope you won't think my society will spoil the trip for you."

"Oh, no, of course, I shall be delighted to have you," said the beauty, in tones so cold and with such a vicious glance at Rhoda and such a frown of dismay at Jack that it was impossible not to understand that the announcement was a terrible shock to her. "And when did you make up your mind to this? Rather sudden, isn't it?"

"Not too sudden, I hope."

"Oh, no, of course not. It will be delightful."

Lady Sarah's manner was not encouraging. She at once changed the subject and began to talk about other things; and nothing more was said about the proposed trip until the ladies left the room. Then Lady Sarah seized Rhoda almost roughly by the arm, and asked:

"You had heard about this horrible Egypt trip, I suppose, before me?"

"Yes. Sir Robert mentioned it to me this afternoon."

"Ah! You encouraged him in the wild idea, perhaps?"

"Oh, Lady Sarah, is it a wild idea on his part, to think that he would like to spend the winter with you instead of away from you?"

"Oh, pray don't expect me to be sentimental. There's nothing I hate so much. Egypt may be all very well for those who like it, and to play Darby and Joan may be a very nice way of spending one's time before twenty-five and after fifty-five. But the years between those ages are better filled one's own way; and I can assure you that, if you are leading Sir Robert to believe that he will find me a pleasant travelling companion, you are making a sad mistake."

The acerbity of her tones frightened Rhoda, who would fain have believed the breach between husband and wife to be less wide than it really was. She said nothing to this. Lady Sarah looked at her keenly. She did not want to quarrel with Rhoda, who knew too much to be treated anything but well.

"You are a dear creature," she said suddenly, as Rhoda said nothing to her tirade, "but I really do wish you would confine yourself to being sweet to Caryl, and nice to Sir Robert, and that you wouldn't try to make silk out of spiders' webs. That is what your labour is, when you try to make a humdrum domestic animal of an insignificant insect like me."

She laughed lightly, and said no more about it. But Rhoda saw, as Lady Sarah flitted across to the piano and began to play lively music with her usual disregard of time and liberal allowance of wrong notes, that she meant mischief.

Minnie was a silent spectator of this scene, although perhaps, being curled up in an awkward position in a sofa at the far end of the drawing-room, she did not hear all that the ladies said.

No sooner did the gentlemen come in than Lady Sarah sprang up from the piano with a light in her eyes, and going straight to her husband led him out into the conservatory, and thence through the library into the study, where she stood up in front of him with her hands behind her, and challenged him fiercely.

"Who put this silly Egypt idea into your head, tell me that?" she asked imperiously, looking up with flashing brown eyes into his grave face.

It was still much graver than usual, by the way.

"What does it matter how the idea came to me," said he gently, "if it be a good one?"

"But it isn't. It's a very bad one indeed," said she hotly. "The absurdity of your giving up your cosy home which you love, to travel about with me! When you know very well I can take care of myself."

Then he spoke with a sudden change of manner that silenced and alarmed her.

"My dear," he said, as he held her arm in a grip which made it impossible for her to think of escape, "that is just what I am asking myself: whether you can take care of yourself, such care as my darling wife ought to take."

"What—do you mean?" panted out the beauty, in sudden terror.

"I mean that it has been borne in upon me, by circumstances to which I need not refer, that I have not been as mindful of your best interests or my own, or our boy's, as I ought to have been. I have begun to realise that a woman as beautiful and charming as you are, one so much younger, too, than her husband, ought not to be left so much to herself as you have been left. I ask you to forgive me, and to help me to do my duty better for the future."

He bent down to kiss her, but she resisted him, holding herself stiffly away and flashing indignant glances at him.

"I know who has put these absurd ideas into your head," she cried angrily. "I know who it is that has come between us, pretending to be so very good, and filling your mind, poisoning it with her wicked suspicions."

"Suspicions!"

Sir Robert's tone changed, grew hard, stern, alarming. Lady Sarah looked up at him with sudden shyness.

"What has she said about me?" she asked in a trembling voice.

But he was staring down intently into her face, as if he would read the very soul behind it.

"She has urged me to take more care of you, that's all," said he in a strange, wistful tone.

"I knew it was to her interference that I owed this disgraceful piece of impertinence," she cried shrilly.

"Impertinence! Do you accuse me of that, in suggesting that I wish to travel with you?"

"N—n—o, of course not," whispered Lady Sarah. "I mean it is impertinent of her to tell you wicked lies about me. It's malicious, infamous! What has she said?"

Suddenly she stood very erect, looking up with keen inquiry into his face.

He took up the challenge at last.

"She has said nothing. But I see for myself that—you pass too much of your time with Jack!"

He was ashamed of himself as he uttered the words; it was horrible to have to hint at any fault in her. But he was driven into a corner, and had not enough finesse to avoid blurting out the truth.

She burst into a broken, mirthless, angry laugh.

"Oh indeed! I see too much of Jack! I pass too much time with him! And what of Miss Pembury? I don't complain of your affection for her, or of the way in which she has wormed herself into your confidence, until your first thought is to take advice from her, even in a matter which concerns your wife."

He stammered, surprised at her swift retort. But she went on, volubly, haughtily.

"If I don't complain about your fondness for her, or about her insinuating herself into your affections and those of my own child, I really don't see why you should make horrible insinuations about your own ward."

He silenced her sternly.

"You forget yourself," said he in a voice which frightened her by its sudden unexpected assumption of masculine powers and rights. "No one knows better than you do that I am incapable of disloyalty to you, that my only fault towards you has been my weakness in being unable to resist or control you. Never let me hear a word of this trivial pretence of jealousy again. You are not jealous, you could not be. God forgive me for saying it, but I only wish you were!"

The heartfelt emotion which thrilled in these words would have softened a woman less self-willed, less hardened in her own caprices than Lady Sarah. As it was, she was only frightened, not touched to tenderness. It was he who was ashamed of the feelings which threatened to overpower him.

Ashamed of his own weakness, and fearing that he was only irritating instead of softening her, he suddenly let her go, and raising her hand to his lips, pressed one tender kiss upon it and then, turning sharply away, felt in his pocket for the keys of his gallery and went out of the study.

Lady Sarah listened a few moments, until she heard the key turn in the gallery door, and knew that her husband had shut himself in with his treasures for the evening.

Then she quickly dried her own eyes, arranged her slightly disordered hair at a tiny gold-mounted mirror which she wore, with other pretty trifles, on her long neck-chain, and with a sigh, found her way quickly to the drawing-room, where Jack Rotherfield, looking rather anxious and perturbed, was affecting to try to flirt with Minnie.

Lady Sarah beckoned him to her side as soon as she entered the room, and with an angry glance at Rhoda, who was pretending to read a book to hide the emotion from which she was suffering, whispered hurriedly:

"It's she who has put him up to this. You must get round her!"

CHAPTER XIV.
JACK ROTHERFIELD'S EFFRONTERY

LADY SARAH was nothing if not versatile. She had scarcely whispered these warning words to Jack Rotherfield when she danced across the room to Minnie, and laughingly said:

"You lazy girl! You're always curled up in a chair or a couch, and you never take any exercise. Come out and race me to the end of the grass path. I don't believe you've been out all day."

The ruse was not a very subtle one, and Rhoda and the sharp-eyed Minnie knew at once that Lady Sarah desired to leave the other two together.

Rhoda, however, walked at once quickly towards the door, with the intention of avoiding an unpleasant *tête-à-tête*.

But of course Jack Rotherfield was far too much accustomed to getting his own way with the ladies not to know how, in the most charming and winning manner, to frustrate her purpose.

Springing across the room with the agility of a boy, he stood, laughing, before the door, and said:

"No, no, you shan't run away like that, as if I were an ogre. I have forgiven you your unkindness to me this morning, and in return you must forgive me if I was not very civil."

But his effrontery, instead of succeeding with her, made her angry. Looking him steadily in the face, she said, her eyes flashing the steely fire that only blue eyes can show:

"You may be able to forgive me, Mr. Rotherfield, but it's too late to ask me to forgive *you*."

For a moment he was confounded, but he quickly recovered himself.

"What do you mean?" he said.

"Must I say it? Remember, I shall have a good deal to say," said she, below her breath.

He cast at her a look which frightened her, so full of undisguised malice was it.

"Say it and let us have it out," he said defiantly.

"Well, you stole the picture; you were taking it up to town—to sell. And it was you, no doubt, who robbed Sir Robert of his snuff-boxes also. There is no injustice in taking that for granted."

"Indeed! Now *I* should have thought there was the cruellest injustice in accusing any man of a theft which you couldn't prove up to the hilt."

"Very well. We will leave out the matter of the snuff-boxes then. You can't deny that you stole the picture."

96

"I do deny it. If I had a hand in it, you know for whom it was done. You know whose extravagance has to be paid for, somehow or other; and that a man, placed in such a position as I, is forced to choose between betraying one of his friends or the other. I stood by the woman. What else could I do?"

Rhoda was aghast at the effrontery of this confession. There might be some truth in it, though she could not but think that his extravagance was quite as likely to have led up to the robbery as that of Lady Sarah.

In any case, his excuse was, of course, thoroughly bad.

"You presume to tell me you were in the right in helping a wife to rob her husband!" she cried.

"In the circumstances, what else could I do?"

"Anything else, of course," Rhoda retorted contemptuously. "Sir Robert is the most generous man in the world."

Jack raised his eyebrows.

"Oh, have you found him so?" sneered he.

Rhoda grew red, but did not affect to notice the sneer.

"He is quite unable to deny his wife anything she asks for. If she had gone to him with a full statement of the amount she wanted, he would have given it to her at once."

"Your experience of him, unfortunately, scarcely tallies with that of his wife," said Jack coolly. "She begged him to let her have some money, and he refused."

"I don't believe it. At least he would ask her for the amount of her debts and then undertake to pay them."

"And is that what you call confidence, generosity. To treat her like a child, to make her give an account of every penny?"

It struck Rhoda forcibly, as she listened to this indictment of the baronet, that Jack had been trying to get money for his own expenses out of his late guardian by means of Lady Sarah: it was a shrewd guess, and Jack saw what was in her mind.

"I think it is quite permissible, with a wife inclined to extravagance," said Rhoda. "In any case, for an outsider to interfere, and to try to take by stealth from a husband what cannot be got from him openly, is an infamous thing. You profess to love Sir Robert, and you show your gratitude by leading his wife into crime. It is frightful, disgraceful."

"And you have told Sir Robert this extraordinary story?"

"Of course not. But I am thankful to see that he knows at last that he has trusted Lady Sarah too much, and I hope he will make it impossible for her to stoop to such conduct in the future."

Jack shot at her a look so full of active malevolence that Rhoda was startled. A low cry escaped her lips, and instinctively she glanced down at his scarred right hand, which Jack as instinctively concealed.

Her knowledge that the affair they were discussing was only a part, and the least important part, of an ugly maze of wrong-doing which she did not dare even to allude to, suddenly seized her imagination so vividly that she sank into a chair, feeling faint and sick with the weight of guilt which seemed to be pressing down upon herself.

For was not this man guilty also of the death of the butler Langton? And what was the guilty secret that lay under that outrage?

For a moment they were both silent, Jack looking askance at her with an expression of intense malignity on his handsome countenance, and Rhoda for the time incapable of speech, and almost of movement.

Then there struck upon their ears the sound of deliberate footsteps in the hall, and both became aware, at the same moment, that the footsteps were those of Sir Robert, and that there was an unwonted firmness in his tread.

The next moment, as Jack glanced apprehensively at the door, it opened, and Sir Robert came in.

He was as white as the dead, and his mild eyes were burning with a strange and sombre fire. Rhoda held her breath, for she knew that, in the short time that had elapsed since he left them, he had made some momentous discovery.

"Miss Pembury," said he, in a voice which hurt her, so cold and cutting were its tones, "will you leave us for ten minutes?" And then he looked full in her face with an expression which told her more than words could have done. She knew that he was in possession, if not of the worst there was to be known, at any rate of enough to break a man's heart.

She hesitated a moment; she would have liked to try to say some word to mitigate the horror of the shock he had received. But what could she say?

Closing her lips, and casting at him one look full of reverence and sympathy and pity, she went, tottering, out of the room, and left the two men together.

With a swift movement, altogether unlike his usual leisurely actions, Sir Robert flung upon a little table near him a folded piece of paper.

"We have some notes to take, both of us," he said, in a steady voice which sounded quite unlike his own. "Here is a pencil for you, and here is mine. I'll give you half this paper, and I'll keep half. Lend me your penknife."

He was bending down over the paper, and holding out his hand, not looking at Jack.

There was a moment's hesitancy on the part of the young man, and then he produced his penknife from his pocket. It was a neat little gold-cased affair, very flat, and with two blades. He opened one of these, and handed the knife to Sir Robert.

The baronet took it from him, but instead of using it as a paper-knife, as he had appeared to wish to do, he turned his back to Jack, and taking something from his own pocket, looked down earnestly at what he held in his hands. Then he turned without a word or a cry, and held under Jack's eyes the penknife, with the second blade opened.

This second blade was broken, having lost about half an inch. In Sir Robert's other hand was the missing piece of steel.

Holding the penknife in one hand and the piece of broken blade in the other, the baronet looked up steadily into the eyes of the young man, and said:

"I picked up this broken blade under the space in the wall where my Romney used to hang." Jack started violently, in spite of all his caution. The baronet went on in an awful voice: "It was your penknife which cut the picture out of its frame. It was you who stole it. Deny it if you can."

For a moment Jack was too much overwhelmed to speak.

Then, recovering himself, he stammered out:

"I don't understand. Some one must have stolen my penknife. I—I am sur—prised that you can accuse me of stealing your picture."

But he had scarcely got to the end of his stammering, halting speech when Sir Robert, with a vigour and muscular strength of which the younger man would never have dreamt him to be possessed, flung himself upon him, and dragging him across the floor, threw him violently upon the couch by the fireplace, and holding him down, in a grip that grew tighter every moment, stared into his face with eyes that blazed like those of an enraged lion.

"The picture! The picture! What do I care for the picture? What would a thousand pictures matter? What I want to know, what I *will* know is—what have you robbed me of besides? You are a thief, a pitiful thief, but I could forgive you that. But you didn't do this thing alone: you had a companion, an accomplice. Who was it? Who was it? Tell me, tell me!"

And as he spoke, with a terrible look, he clutched Jack Rotherfield by the throat and forced the guilty eyes to meet his own.

CHAPTER XV.
SELF-ACCUSATIONS

JACK ROTHERFIELD made no reply; indeed the hands of Sir Robert were pressing so tightly on his throat that he could scarcely have spoken if he had wished to do so.

For a few minutes the two men glared each at the other; Sir Robert pale with fierce anger, in deadly earnest, and probably unconscious how strong was his grip. Jack gasping, gurgling, perhaps affecting more inconvenience than he actually experienced, in order to gain time, and to think of an answer to satisfy the incensed husband.

But before the silence was broken, while Jack still lay struggling in the fierce grip of his captor, there was a sound on the terrace, a scream, a flutter of drapery, and Lady Sarah dashed into the room.

"What is it? Oh, what is it? What are you doing? You are killing him!" she cried, as she flew across the room and tried to drag her husband away.

But he shook her off almost roughly, and said, in a tone he had never used to her before:

"Go away. We must settle this between ourselves, he and I."

But she would not go. Guessing now that some terrible revelation had been made to Sir Robert, and that a crisis had been reached, she came back when she had been repulsed, and throwing herself between the two men, stared up into her husband's face, and said:

"Tell me what has happened. Tell me, tell me. I must, I will know."

Sir Robert relaxed his hold on Jack Rotherfield, seized his wife by the shoulders, and looked her full in the face with penetrating, angry eyes.

"Why do you ask these questions? You know what it is I've found out. I know that you and he were engaged together last night in robbing me. What have you to say for yourself? Answer me if you can."

There was, under all his ferocity, a hungry look of longing, an expression of strained eagerness to hear something from her lips which would mitigate the harshness of the sentence he must pass upon her.

There was silence for a few moments. Jack Rotherfield had risen hastily from the couch, and was standing, panting, a little behind Sir Robert, in the hope of being able to catch Lady Sarah's eye.

But the baronet, now wholly alert and as keen to suspicion as a man could be, foiled this attempt at an exchange of looks or signs, by turning her round, so that she faced Jack, who did not dare to move away.

Lady Sarah, sobbing, tearful, trembling, looked up with a sudden impulse of daring.

"Well," she almost shrieked out, dashing away her tears, "and what if I did? I wanted money, and you wouldn't give it me. I begged you to let me have some, and all you would let me have was twenty pounds. Twenty pounds! After spending thousands on your pictures! I know it was wrong to steal your Romney; I know it was theft. But I didn't know what else to do. I didn't know where to turn. I made up my mind to take the picture, partly to pay my bills, and partly to have my revenge on you for being so mean to me. And Jack found out what I was going to do. And he tried to stop me, but I wouldn't be stopped. So he helped me instead. The blame is all mine, all mine. He didn't want to do it. I took the snuff-boxes myself, without his knowing anything about it. I got hold of the keys Miss Pembury used to take care of, and I took the snuff-boxes and put back the keys. There. That's the story, all, all of it."

Her eyes were dry and burning by this time, and she gazed up boldly, defiantly, at her husband.

He was plainly uncertain what to do, what to believe. Lady Sarah pressed her advantage.

"Of course I know I've done wrong, and I won't ask you to forgive me. I only ask you to put the blame upon me, and not upon Jack, who only helped me because he couldn't let me be caught by myself."

Sir Robert made an impatient movement. Such magnanimity made him incredulous.

"There's no excuse for either of you," he said. "You both knew me."

"Yes, and I knew you wouldn't help me, for I asked you, and you refused."

"I have never refused to help you. I offered to pay your bills."

"You refused to give me money for myself. You wanted to treat me like a child. You showed that you distrusted me. Well, who is to blame, then, if I showed that I was not to be trusted? I was only treating you as you evidently expected me to treat you, wasn't I?"

Her husband would not look at her. He was puzzled, sick at heart with mistrust much deeper than any he had betrayed to her. Was this all that he had to learn, that these two had combined together to rob him of his picture? That was the question which was agitating him, and to which he dared not as yet seek an answer.

The horrible secret which they had kept from him, this theft by which his own wife had, in conjunction with another man, sought to revenge herself upon him and to rob him at the same time, was such an unexpected revelation to the loyal-hearted and generous man, that on learning it he seemed to have stepped into a new world, where everything round him wore a fresh aspect, and where those nearest and dearest to him were transformed into shapes scarcely human.

He heard her lame and audacious attempt at defence, and waved his hand as if to ward off a blow.

"I can't argue with you," he said. "The whole thing is too shocking, too humiliating to us both, to us all."

"Very well. I don't ask you to forgive me. You've never understood me. I was never a suitable wife for you, and we can't do each other justice," said Lady Sarah. "However, we need not trouble one another any longer. I'll get back your snuff-boxes if I can."

"No, no. I don't want them back. I don't want ever to see again anything to remind me of this terrible day."

Lady Sarah threw out her hands in a gesture of helpless despair.

"Very well. You shall not see anything to remind you of it, if I can help it. Of course for one thing, you don't want to see me again."

He looked at her sternly, but she would not meet his eyes. She went on quickly:

"I'll go back to my father's house. Whatever has to be arranged for the future you can arrange with him and with my mother. I don't care what becomes of me. I've not been treated properly: I've been treated as if I were a doll. My life has been spoilt, and I have been sacrificed to other people's blundering. Very well. I'll do what I can to efface myself, and let us hear no more about it. You've got back your picture, and that's all you wanted. It will console you for the loss of a wife whom you never cared to try to understand."

She grew more and more excited as she went on, and ended by throwing herself on a sofa in a paroxysm of hysterical weeping.

Sir Robert stood motionless in the middle of the room, while Jack Rotherfield eyed him stealthily from near the window.

His wife's wild accusations only affected him in proportion as they seemed to support or to refute the idea of some graver guilt than theft. He would not look at her, would not let himself be softened.

"I will take the night," said he gravely, "to consider what to do." He turned abruptly to his wife. "You had better go upstairs at once," added he, "and stay in your room until the morning."

She sat up, indignant.

"Am I to be kept a prisoner?" she asked. "Why not send for the police and give me in charge at once?"

"You will stay in your room," said he, unmoved by her words, "until I send for you in the morning."

"I see. I am to consider myself in custody. And pray, who is to be my gaoler? Not Miss Pembury. I won't be watched by that girl. I suppose now that you are going to get rid of me, you will arrange for her to stay here."

Sir Robert made no answer. But Jack struck in, anxious not to have Rhoda's influence to combat as well as that of the baronet. Although he had failed to make his peace with her that evening, he knew that she had not, so far, told the worst that she had to tell, and it was worth an effort to try to keep her mouth shut, if only on that affair of ten years ago to which, as he knew, she had a clue.

So he suddenly struck into the conversation with an appearance of great magnanimity.

"Miss Pembury must not go away. She doesn't like me, I know, but she is a good woman and she can be trusted. If you have to quarrel with me, Sir Robert, I hope you won't vent your displeasure on either of the ladies. Sarah has done wrong, and I did worse wrong in helping her over the picture. I'm sorry and I'm ashamed. I know nothing can excuse her or me. Send me away, but don't quarrel with her. Forgive her. She has never done anything to offend you till now, and Miss Pembury will take her part, I'm sure. I'll go away to-night, if you like, on condition you let me take all the blame. Indeed I ought to do so."

This magnanimity did not appear greatly to impress Sir Robert. The terrible doubts which assailed him, indeed, made all other considerations seem of minor importance.

But this address, if it did not impress the baronet, had its effect upon Lady Sarah. She was quick to jump to the conclusion that she was to take her cue from Jack, and to keep "in" with Rhoda, if she could. So she said:

"Jack is right, Robert. You must keep Miss Pembury, if only for Caryl's sake. As for poor me, I don't count, do I, now? But at least if you are going to send me away, let me have a talk with Rhoda first. Perhaps I can explain things to her better than to you, and if she believes me, why, I suppose you will."

Sir Robert frowned. He did not like the tone which he noted in his wife's speech, through which there seemed to run an undercurrent of sarcasm which offended and distressed him.

Lady Sarah, having made up her mind what to do, was already, in her impulsive fashion, on the way to carry it out.

"I will go straight to her," she said, "and ask her to persuade you, not to forgive me, if you don't want to forgive, but to do me justice. You are not doing me justice now."

"I am trying to," said he gravely.

Lady Sarah was at the door.

"Perhaps, with her help, you will succeed," said she with some appearance of dignity, as she swept out of the room, throwing at Jack a glance of intelligence which implied that she was following his lead.

Sir Robert did not condescend to look at Jack again, but turning towards him, with his eyes averted, he said:

"I'll see you in the morning."

And with that he left the room and went upstairs, determined to keep watch himself, in order to prevent any meeting between his wife and Jack before the latter was safely got out of the house.

Already he was hoping that things were not so bad as he had at first been inclined to fear. The spirit shown by his wife had been, he thought, a hopeful sign. Bad as her conduct had been in robbing her own husband, he was hoping that might prove to be the worst, and that even that was rather the result of malice and mischief than depravity.

Certainly it was hard to reconcile this view of her behaviour with common sense. But Sir Robert shrank from the alternative. Going straight upstairs, with the intention of playing gaoler, as his wife had called it, to the extent of preventing any interview between her and Jack, he saw Lady Sarah going into Rhoda's room.

This was just what he would have wished, and he went on to his own apartment, which was next to that of his wife, without affecting to see her.

Rhoda, who had fled upstairs in an agony of apprehension when Sir Robert came into the drawing-room and asked her to retire, sprang to her feet when she heard Lady Sarah's impatient and haughty voice asking for admittance.

The wilful beauty rushed into the room like a whirlwind, a habit of hers when she was excited, and standing in the middle of the floor, gazed for a few moments defiantly at Rhoda, who had risen to receive her visitor.

Rhoda saw at once that a crisis had been reached in the domestic history of the ill-matched pair. Lady Sarah's face was flushed, her eyes were red, her hair was disordered. Her gown of clinging rose-coloured satin was crumbled and soiled, and in every feature of her face, in every fold of her dress were signs of the disturbance of the past half-hour.

"I hope you are satisfied now, Miss Pembury, with the result of your well-meant advice to my husband, about his treatment of me!" she cried in a voice shrill with emotion, as she played nervously with her rings, and flashed indignant glances into Rhoda's frank face. "You've roused suspicions in him which he ought to be ashamed of. He has made an awful scene, first with Jack and then with me, and the end will be the break up of the household."

"What scene?" asked Rhoda hoarsely.

"Sir Robert professes to have found out that the picture was stolen by—by Jack, and so I had to say that I was the culprit. Now he has given us till to-morrow, when, I suppose, I shall have to go back to my parents, and poor Jack will be driven away too, of course."

Rhoda was desperate, so she refused to be apologetic, or even sympathetic.

"Well, he couldn't do better than that, at least, Lady Sarah, and you know that as well as I do."

To her intense surprise, Lady Sarah took this boldly expressed opinion much better than she had expected. Staring intently into Rhoda's face, she asked in a low voice:

"Do you really mean that, that you think he ought to be sent away? Tell me why. Tell me why."

"I think he has had a very bad influence upon you, Lady Sarah."

The baronet's wife took this remark also in fairly good part. It was easier, at any rate, to discuss this matter with another woman than with Sir Robert. She took a seat near the dressing-table, and signed to Rhoda to sit too. Then she leaned on her hand, and looked her steadily in the face.

"You think, I suppose," said she coolly, "that I am fonder of Jack than I ought to be."

This was such unexpected frankness that Rhoda stammered, not quite prepared with a reply. Lady Sarah nodded sagely.

"Of course in a way you are right. I confess that I've always liked Jack better than any other man, much better, for instance, than I've ever liked Sir Robert."

"Oh, hush! pray don't say such things!"

Lady Sarah's pretty face grew mutinous.

"Why shouldn't I say them? You have always known the truth so far, and it would be only cant to pretend you hadn't. Come, Miss Pembury, be honest. You first knew me ten years ago. Didn't you know, even then, that I liked Jack best? If you didn't, you ought to have known. For I'm sure everybody else did."

"Well, even if I did, of course I took it for granted, when I found you married to a man so good and so generous, and so devoted to you, that you were fond of him."

"You should never take anything for granted, with a woman like me. I don't think even Sir Robert took so much for granted as you seem to have done. A man thinks only of getting the woman he likes best to marry him, you know; he never asks himself whether he can make her love him. That's what *he* takes for granted. Sometimes, no doubt, he's right; sometimes, he's wrong. Sir Robert was wrong."

"Oh, don't. I don't like to hear."

"But I want to tell you. Look here, Miss Pembury. We are not great friends, you and I. You don't like me very much, and perhaps I don't appreciate you properly. My husband doesn't think I do, I know."

Rather shocked by this mingled cynicism and honesty, Rhoda was yet interested, fascinated. Lady Sarah could always command any one's interest and attention when she chose to take the trouble. And as she talked, looking the while as pretty as a picture by Greuze in spite of her recent tears, Rhoda could not help her own heart going out to the wayward creature, who talked so simply, and who seemed so frank.

"But, at any rate, as we're both women, we ought to be able to understand each other, if we try. I want you to understand me. Not from any wish to make out a case for myself, but because I want some one to know, and to remember afterwards, just what Sir Robert is doing in driving Jack Rotherfield away. He will have to go, of course. Probably Sir Robert will make a pretence of forgiving me for my share in the picture affair, and I shall be allowed to remain here, as an act of distinguished clemency. But I don't want to remain. If Jack, who is my friend, is sent away, and I am kept here as a sort of prisoner on parole, I might as well die at once. Of what use will my life be to me? If I am not trusted to have my own friends, if I am to find my amusement in Sir Robert's stuffed birds, why should I take the trouble to live at all?"

"But Sir Robert isn't so unreasonable. He wants you to be happy, and as he sees that you can't be happy long at home, he is ready to take you abroad."

"But I don't want to go—with him. Oh, don't look shocked. I've only dared to be so candid with you because I'm really quite innocent of anything worse than being bored to death by my own husband. You need not tell me he is good and generous, and all that. I've no doubt he is. But I can't work myself up into enthusiasm about such negative qualities. I want something more piquant, more exciting, in a man than that. If only I'd been allowed to go on in my own way, all would have been right. I wasn't a very good wife, perhaps, nor an absolutely perfect mother. But I never did anything wrong, or shocking, nothing worse than amuse myself in my own way with my own friends. Now you, with the best intentions, I'm sure, have made that impossible, what can you expect of me? Do you think I shall settle down at once to spectacles and knitting? Do you imagine that Sir Robert will at once find me an ideal companion, say, for a wet day? Oh, no, you know better than that. Well, what do you expect then?"

Rhoda answered with diffidence. Lady Sarah could put her own case well, of course, and it was evident that she quite believed all that she was saying. Rhoda began to doubt, herself, whether the upheaval in the domestic life at the Mill-house would not result in a change for the worse all round, and not for the better.

"Couldn't you meet Sir Robert ever such a little way?" she suggested timidly.

"How? Just tell me how."

"Would it really be such an infliction to take a journey with him to a country you have never visited? You would stay at the best hotels, enjoy yourself in your own way, only with your husband looking on, instead of right out of it. I'm sure you could trust him not to interfere with your amusements; all he would ask would be to be your companion, your protector."

Lady Sarah screwed up her pretty features expressively. It was plain that the prospect had no charms for her. But she was silent a moment and then she threw out her arms with a sigh.

"That's what I shall have to do, I suppose," said she. "But it will be horrid—for both of us. Well," she rose and nodded casually without putting out her hand: "at least now you understand me better than you did, even if you can't find any excuses for my shocking behaviour."

She was quite her old self again, mocking, laughing, contemptuous, charming.

Rhoda wondered, when she was alone, whether there was any possibility of touching her heart, or of making her realise her responsibilities in life.

She seemed to be absolutely without any sense of them; and although Rhoda was inclined to believe her account of the relations between her and Jack, realising as she did that there were no depths in the wayward woman, no heart-yearnings to be satisfied, she asked herself, in a kind of terror, whether such negative virtues were not even more hopeless to deal with than would have been the stormy passion of a guilty love.

CHAPTER XVI.
A FRUSTRATED ELOPEMENT

On the following morning Sir Robert went to Jack's room before that young man was up, and sitting on the edge of his bed, gave him such a searching catechism, ending with such a severe lecture, that his late ward was surprised at the thoroughness with which the baronet, his fears once roused, tackled the subject of his wife's flirtation.

The result of this was satisfactory in the main to Sir Robert. Jack appeared to be perfectly frank and only slightly ashamed of himself. He protested that he and Lady Sarah had never been more to each other than sympathetic companions and devoted friends, and that, while he admitted he was fonder of her than he had ever been of any woman, they had never exceeded the limits of innocent flirtation; and Jack reminded the baronet that he must have been aware, all this time, that they did flirt.

Sir Robert scarcely knew how to meet this.

It was true that his wife had openly flirted with Jack before him; but coquetry was ingrain in her nature, and when she had nobody else to amuse herself with, she even, upon occasion, coquetted, much to his delight, with her husband himself.

The upshot of the conversation was that he obtained from Jack a solemn promise to go away without an attempt to communicate with Lady Sarah, and to travel abroad for a time, undertaking the while not to correspond with her.

Upon this promise Jack was allowed to leave the house at once, under an appearance of perfect amity with its master; and the simple-minded baronet congratulated himself on having got out of a difficulty and saved his brilliant wife from further danger, in a fairly satisfactory manner.

When Lady Sarah came downstairs, she was met by her husband, who escorted her into the morning-room, and told her, very gently and without any further appearance of anger or resentment, that he and Jack had talked over the matter of their conversation of the previous night, and that they had both come to the conclusion that the best thing to be done was that all relations between the young man and his friends at the Mill-house should be broken off for the present.

Lady Sarah, sitting by the window with her lips compressed and her hands tightly clasped, listened in dead silence. When he had finished she paused, and receiving no reply, at length said:

"Well! I hope you're satisfied that we've done the best thing possible to bury this unhappy affair of the loss of the picture?"

"Oh, quite," said she lightly, in a hard, scoffing tone. "Jack and I are each put in a corner, and bidden not to turn our faces round from the wall to look at each other. Nothing could be better."

"I wish you wouldn't take it like that, my dear. You must realise that you have been playing with your reputation," he said.

"Oh, hang my reputation. What's the use of having a husband at all if his presence isn't sufficient security for his wife's good behaviour?"

It was "a nasty one," and it was meant to be so. Sir Robert drew back, wounded.

"It's by your own wish," said he rather drily, "that our relations are not closer than they are."

"Certainly. And how long is this arrangement to last? How long is it going to take my invalid reputation to get well again?"

Sir Robert frowned uneasily.

"Do you mean that you want to know when Jack can come here again?"

"Yes. People will talk, you know. And instead of my intercourse with him being looked upon, as it always was, and as it rightly was, as perfectly innocent, people will put their heads together, and talk about what Sir Robert 'found out.'"

"We must risk something," said Sir Robert shortly. "We risk as little as we can. I want, if you please, your word of honour that you will hold no sort of communication with him until I give you leave to do so. That you will neither see him nor write to him nor receive letters from him."

"Oh, I must promise, I suppose. Though it's rather hard upon him, considering that the picture affair was my fault, and not his at all."

"He must expect to take his share of the blame," said Sir Robert. "And now, my dear, since we shall be more dependent upon each other's society, I hope you will not find me very exacting or very tiresome."

His tone was full of tenderness, but it met with no response from Lady Sarah. Perhaps, in the circumstances, it was scarcely likely that the spoilt beauty would receive his overtures graciously. She rose, shrugged her shoulders, and saying briefly, "Oh, I shall be very good," she went out of the room forgetting that she had had no breakfast.

Sir Robert looked depressed and uneasy. It was not a good beginning, certainly, of the happy domestic life he had begun to hope for.

Before the day was over it became plain that Lady Sarah had thought the matter out, and had made up her mind what part to play.

She showed herself wonderfully bright, lively, charming, not only to her husband, but to Rhoda, so that Minnie raised her eyebrows, and, after making futile guesses as to what could have happened, and as to the reason of Jack Rotherfield's abrupt disappearance, expressed the opinion that her aunt was too amiable to be able to "keep it up."

But she was wrong. Day after day passed and still Lady Sarah was sweet-tempered and bright, playful with her husband, amusing with Rhoda and Minnie, and affectionate to Caryl.

Sir Robert was delighted at this new phase of his wife's character, and congratulated himself, dear, simple man, on the accident which had seemed so terrible at the time, which had given him an opportunity of putting matters on a sound and safe footing.

But Rhoda and Minnie, with their acute feminine perception of character, detected something forced in Lady Sarah's laughter, something insincere and hollow in her amiability. She chatted with a vivacity which was almost feverish, and her laughter did not, to their keen ears, ring quite true.

And then Rhoda could not help noticing that Lady Sarah became suddenly much more fond of taking walks by herself than formerly, and saw her coming out of a little newspaper shop in the High Street, where it was very unlikely that she would buy either books or stationery.

Rhoda, ashamed of herself for the thought, came nevertheless to the conclusion that Lady Sarah went there to get letters which she could not safely receive at home.

The suspicion was a dreadful one to bear, for if she was right, Rhoda saw that Lady Sarah had not scrupled to break her promise to her husband as soon as it was made.

Rhoda changed her own line of conduct a little, gave up, as much as possible, her share of Sir Robert's work, in the hope that his wife would take it up. The only result was, however, that, used to Rhoda's orderly ways, poor Sir Robert soon got into a hopeless muddle with his notes and manuscripts, when he was thus suddenly left once more to his own devices, while Lady Sarah secretly enjoyed his discomfiture.

Rhoda, meanwhile, kept almost entirely to Caryl's rooms, except when he went out, when she never failed to accompany him. She scarcely ever got a moment to herself, and she had been thus almost confined to the house for a fortnight, when, running down the hill to the pillar-box at the corner to post a letter to one of her sisters, she caught sight of a motor-car turning into a side-road, and asked herself, with a horrible shock of suspicion and surprise, whether it was not that of Jack Rotherfield.

It was dusk, and she knew there was a possibility that she might have been mistaken; but the presence of Jack in the neighbourhood, in spite of his promise and Lady Sarah's, was only too probable, and much against her own inclination, Rhoda felt obliged to keep a look out for eventualities.

When she got home, she was surprised to find Lady Sarah in Caryl's room, sitting by the boy, holding his hand, and speaking to him with much more than her usual kindness and sweetness.

Rhoda held her breath, and her cheeks blanched with a growing fear. Was this only a coincidence, the reappearance of Jack Rotherfield, and the sudden undergrowth in Lady Sarah of something like an ordinary mother's love for her child?

Rhoda could not but ask herself the question; and when Lady Sarah looked up at her quickly, and holding out her hand, said: "Ah, Miss Pembury, I've been trying to interest Caryl, but you are his real mother, and I hope you always will be." Rhoda could scarcely make an audible answer, so strong was her conviction that important events were impending.

Lady Sarah was dressed for dinner, and was looking, Rhoda thought, even handsomer than usual, her eyes being very bright, and her whole countenance suffused with an unusual softness, as if at last she had found out how to feel.

It was with a deep anxiety at her heart that Rhoda quickly made her own toilet, and hurried downstairs. Dinner was now usually a very lively affair, as Lady Sarah's new high spirits seemed always at their highest when she was with her husband and Rhoda together. On this occasion, however, she was scarcely herself. She asked questions without waiting for the answers, and laughed without reason.

And through it all Rhoda noticed with pain that the new affection she had just shown to her boy, whom she had kissed with real heartiness when she left him, was not present in her manner when she addressed her husband.

Sir Robert felt that something was wrong, but evidently did not know what to make of the change in his wife. He asked her rather diffidently if she felt quite well, and was answered quite snappishly in the affirmative.

After dinner Lady Sarah made an excuse of a slight headache to retire to her own rooms, and Rhoda, on the alert, also made an excuse, so that she might be on the watch for developments.

She did not go upstairs, however, but slipping out of the house by the garden door, waited about in the shadow of the trees under the east wall, and kept her eye on the windows of Lady Sarah's rooms.

She could see that some one was flitting about between the three rooms, bedroom, dressing-room and boudoir. Then there was an interval, and Rhoda presently saw Lady Sarah, in her motor-coat, hat and veil, come quickly and stealthily out of the house, carrying her travelling bag in her hand.

The girl could scarcely suppress an exclamation of horror. She remained, however, shivering and without uttering a sound, until Lady Sarah came close to her and put out her hand to open the side-gate which led into the road.

As she did so, she uttered a soft whistle.

And the sound was echoed from the other side of the wall.

The key was in the lock, when Rhoda sprang forward and touched Lady Sarah on the hand.

"Don't go," she whispered hoarsely. "Oh, Lady Sarah, think of your boy! Come back, come back!"

Lady Sarah had sprung away from her, and Rhoda, commanding the door in the wall, stood erect, blocking the way through.

"What do you mean? What do you want?" she hissed out fiercely.

"I want you to consider what you're doing. I know that Mr. Rotherfield is waiting outside: I know that his car is in one of the side roads."

"You are a spy," cried Lady Sarah.

"I couldn't help myself. I caught sight of the car before dinner, and, and——"

"And you lay in wait for me! I might have expected it!"

"Could I do anything else? I've said nothing to anybody. No one but me has the least idea of anything being wrong."

"There's nothing wrong."

"Oh, there is, there is. You want to run away, from your home, your husband, your child. Lady Sarah, you are fond of Caryl; I could see it in your eyes this evening. You looked at him just as one wanted you always to look. Remember how he looked at you in return, remember the touch of his hand on your cheek. Oh, you wouldn't like him to lose you; you wouldn't like to lose him. Think what you're doing, think, think. You will never be able to come back. How can you be happy, with all your friends cut off, your home wrecked, your own father and mother rendered miserable and ashamed for you. Lady Sarah, you're not heartless; I'll never believe it after seeing you with Caryl to-night. Come back, come back."

Lady Sarah's eyes flashed. She was crying with rage as well as with disappointment and alarm. Rhoda had unintentionally raised her voice during her impassioned entreaty, and Lady Sarah knew that Jack, waiting on the outer side of the wall, must know by this time that their plan was in danger of frustration.

Rhoda, indeed, did not content herself with entreaty. By the interposition of her person between Lady Sarah and the door, she made it impossible for the wilful woman to escape.

For this time, at least, it was plain that the escapade must be given up.

"You will tell Sir Robert, of course," she sobbed out.

"No, no, no. I don't want to make mischief. I want to prevent it. But will you keep your word if you promise not to try to go away again? Tell me, tell me, that you will. Oh, Lady Sarah, you must, you must. The shock of your going away, the scandal, the horror of it, would kill your own boy."

"Nonsense. You'd better let me go and get it over. Sir Robert will soon forget me. Let me pass."

She had flung herself on Rhoda, who, desperate, used her last weapon.

"If you go," she said firmly, "I'll tell Sir Robert what I know about the scarred hand, and Mr. Rotherfield shall be had up for Langton's murder."

"You wretch!"

But though Lady Sarah uttered the word with all the fierceness of which she was capable, she dared not, in the face of this threat, go any further with her wicked plan.

"All right. I give way," she said in a tone of rage and despair.

Rhoda trembling and sick at heart, saw Sir Robert's wife tear off her coat and veil, and hurry back into the house.

Rhoda had gained a victory, but what was the price to be paid? That there would be a reckoning to meet she felt sure, and it was with a heavy sense of foreboding, and with none of the spirits of a conqueror that she in her turn went, slowly and timidly, back to the house.

CHAPTER XVII.
SIR ROBERT'S PLANS

RHODA took care to let Lady Sarah have plenty of time to get inside the house, and to go upstairs, before she followed.

She desired nothing less than another *tête-à-tête* with the enraged and disappointed woman whom she had just saved from disgrace and guilt. For Lady Sarah was not grateful: the last glance she had thrown at the girl who saved her was full of a bitterness which prepared Rhoda for what she had to expect from her.

As Rhoda glided quietly into the hall from the garden, she stopped and tried to draw back, on seeing Sir Robert was standing at the foot of the stairs. Above him, going slowly up, was Lady Sarah with her motor-coat over her arm, and her long veil, which she had untied, dragging on the stairs behind her. There was a sort of defiance in her slow tread, but Rhoda knew that, even if she had exchanged a few words with her husband, she had not had time for a conversation.

The baronet turned on hearing Rhoda, and called to her.

"Miss Pembury!"

Rhoda would fain not have heard, but he repeated her name, and she came reluctantly forward. She guessed that her very looks must be a sort of betrayal, for she was shaking from head to foot.

"You are not well," he said kindly, but still with some sternness in his tone.

"Oh, yes, I am, thank you."

He touched her hand.

"You are cold."

"Yes. I've—I've been out in the grounds."

"Come with me to the study. I want to speak to you."

"Will you excuse me to-night, and speak to me in the morning?" pleaded she.

He shook his head.

"I won't keep you long."

He led the way, and she followed reluctantly enough. When they were both in the study, he pointed to a chair, and as she fell into it rather than sat down, he said:

"Don't be afraid. I have very few questions to ask. I know without asking what has happened."

Rhoda, greatly startled, uttered a sort of sob. He looked at her.

"I've grown more sharp-sighted of late," he said gravely. "I can guess at some things now that I cannot see. I suppose you prevented Lady Sarah from running away?"

It seemed to Rhoda that his tone was stern rather than grateful. She hung her head and said nothing.

"What arguments did you use?"

Rhoda hesitated.

"You said you wouldn't ask me questions," whispered she.

"Well, well, there is no need. I am convinced that my wife was trying to leave her home, and that it was something you did or said that stopped her. But what is the use? You can't mount guard over her for ever. Nor can I. If she has made up her mind to go, what can be done?"

Rhoda sat forward in her chair.

"She won't try again," said she hoarsely.

"What makes you think that?"

"I can only tell you this, that I have a weapon, and that I've used it."

"What weapon?"

Rhoda replied cautiously:

"I have knowledge of something with which she had nothing to do, but which would seriously affect some one else."

"Won't you trust me with it?"

"No, Sir Robert."

"You will make me think it does concern my wife, after all, if you won't tell me what it is."

But Rhoda was firm.

"Oh, no, you can take my word for that. It concerns Mr. Rotherfield, and it is something which he can't afford to have known. But it concerns nobody but him. Now please let me go. I don't want Lady Sarah to think that we are talking about her."

Sir Robert sighed. The discovery of his wife's intention to run away from her home seemed to Rhoda to have affected him very little. She had been prepared for a much stronger display of emotion when he heard the truth. But the fact was that Lady Sarah's conduct had given him so much anxiety of late, and that, in particular, her over-excitement during the past few days had been so marked, that he could not feel much astonishment when he learned what the attempt was to which it had been leading. Nevertheless he was looking very grave, very sad, and very deeply humiliated as Rhoda briefly bade him good-night and went out.

She passed Lady Sarah's door in fear and trembling, dreading that the lady would come out and upbraid her for "conspiring" with Sir Robert against her. But she reached her own room in safety, and without molestation.

Next morning Lady Sarah did not come down to breakfast, and the first anxious thought in Rhoda's mind was that she had carried out her plan of elopement after all.

But before the morning was half over the mistress of the house glided into the morning-room, looking very cold, hard, and resentful, very hollow about the eyes and listless of manner, the mere wreck of the brilliant woman she had been within the past week.

She and Rhoda met with considerable reserve on both sides, as was inevitable. Gone was all kindness on Lady Sarah's part; even her boy's voice addressing her caused no relaxation of her features. She treated him as an interruption, and frowned as she crossed the room at his call. And Rhoda's heart throbbed painfully when she remembered the touching way in which the beauty had spoken to the child on the previous night; when she had shown him a momentary tenderness which was real. It had only been the flicker of a love which absence would soon have extinguished altogether.

The boy looked chilled and disappointed. Remembering the sweetness of her look and touch on the previous night he had been ready with a smile for her, and her coldness pained him and struck him into silence.

There was a painful pause, as they all heard the sound of the steps of Sir Robert in the hall outside. But when he came in, they were all struck by the change in his manner. Instead of being slow and stately, he was brisk and alert. He did not smile as he bade them all good-morning, and even when he stooped to kiss his son, his face was stern and set.

He spoke with a most unusual tone of command as he turned to his wife and said:

"Sarah, I have settled some of the details of our journey abroad already. I want you to go to town with me to-day to buy anything you may want, and to help me as to any details which I may have forgotten."

"I don't want to go abroad," she said sullenly.

These were the first words which the two had exchanged since Sir Robert had become aware of his wife's attempt to run away from him. Rhoda held her breath as she listened, without daring to look up.

There was quite a new tone in Sir Robert's voice, and instead of being all gentleness and kindness to his wife, consulting her convenience and yielding to her wishes, he was laying down the law as to his plans, and quite simply taking her adhesion for granted, just like an ordinary husband.

Her answer did not disconcert him in the least, neither did it appear to have any weight with him.

"I have decided for you this time," he said quietly. "And all that is left for you to do is to fall in with my plans."

Lady Sarah looked up. This was a change indeed.

"Where are you going?" she asked in the same sullen tone as before.

"To Paris first. Then on to Lyons, and Marseilles. I don't think you know Marseilles?"

"No. I don't wish to know it."

"I've no doubt you will like it when you are there."

"I prefer the Riviera."

"You have been there so often. It will be better for you to have a thorough change."

"I don't want a change. You can go to Marseilles and I'll go to Monte Carlo with my mother, as usual."

Sir Robert looked at her with a new determination in his eyes.

"No. I've made my arrangements, and you must fall in with them. You have had your own way about your holiday for a good many winters; now you must give way to mine."

Lady Sarah looked up with hard, mutinous eyes. But there was a look in those of her husband which she could not meet more than a few moments. With an impatient shrug of the shoulders she turned away and walked towards the door.

"The carriage will be round in five minutes," said he. "Please get ready quickly, as we haven't much time to catch the train."

"I should advise you to go alone. I shall be a most dull companion to-day, I can assure you."

"Well, it will be a very proper revenge on your part. For you have found me a dull companion very often, I believe."

Rhoda could have sunk into the earth for shame and surprise at this unpleasant trial of strength between husband and wife, so utterly different from any scene she had ever witnessed between the two before.

Sir Robert held the door open for his wife to pass out, and she ran quickly upstairs. Rhoda wondered whether she would obey the command given her, and waited with a fast beating heart.

Little Caryl, who had been a silent observer, turned to her and beckoned.

"Why is papa so different? And mama too?" he asked under his breath.

And Rhoda could find no answer.

Within the five minutes accorded her Lady Sarah came downstairs hastily and not very carefully dressed, and looking as unlike as possible the brilliant, laughing creature who had been accustomed to impose her will upon all around her.

Like an automaton she went out of the house, got into the victoria, and took her seat in the corner, where she sat without a word to her husband, staring straight before her.

In the train she sat in the same way, burying herself in an illustrated paper, and replying as briefly as possible to his remarks.

But he maintained a perfectly equable demeanour, and it was impossible for her to draw from him a single word either of remonstrance or of impatience.

When they reached town Sir Robert took her straight to a restaurant, and asked her what she would like for luncheon.

"I don't care," she answered coldly. "I don't want any luncheon."

"You will leave me to order it then?" said Sir Robert coolly.

"Oh, yes. Pray don't consult me. I prefer being a cipher."

"Certainly," acquiesced Sir Robert without even a look at her.

And he proceeded to order luncheon for both, taking care to choose such dishes as she preferred.

Lady Sarah had an excellent appetite, and she was hungry. But even a dainty and well chosen repast failed to soften her ill-humour.

"And now," said Sir Robert when they had finished luncheon, "we will go shopping. What shops shall we visit first?"

Lady Sarah laughed.

"Surely you need not consult me. You appear to have made up your mind what I am to buy."

"Very well. If you will leave it to me, I dare say we shall get on very well."

He ordered a taxi, and they drove to one of the best furriers in town. Lady Sarah was passionately fond of furs, and was, he knew, anxious to have a sable cloak for the winter. He asked to have such a garment shown to him, and two magnificent cloaks, either of which might have adorned a princess, were brought and offered to him for inspection.

He turned to his wife.

"Is either of these the sort of thing you had in your mind?"

Ill-tempered as she was, Lady Sarah could scarcely resist the beautiful furs held out before her.

"Perhaps madam would like to try them on, and see which cloak became her the best." For one moment Lady Sarah hesitated, then her ill-temper got the better of her taste again.

"It is not necessary," she said. "They are both very handsome. It is for my husband to choose which he likes best."

"Try them both on," said Sir Robert, without appearing to note the coldness of her tone, which, while it could not be detected by the saleswoman, was quite evident to himself, knowing her moods as he did.

Lady Sarah took off the long coat of purple faced cloth which she was wearing, and obediently put on first one and then the other mantle. Both were beautiful, but the one was much better adapted to her slender little figure than the other.

But when Sir Robert asked her which of the two she would have, she persisted in her exaggerated humility and listlessness, and said it was for him to decide.

Without showing the least impatience, Sir Robert decided for her upon the right mantle, paid the eight hundred pounds which was the price of it, and had it put into the taxi-cab. There was no change in Lady Sarah's expression as she left the shop and heard her husband give the address of a fashionable milliner.

"Am I to get out?" she asked when the taxi stopped at the door.

Quite unmoved, Sir Robert said:

"I think so."

And they entered the shop together.

If there was one place in this world in which Lady Sarah was happier than in another, it was a hat-shop. But in spite of the temptation of the latest creations around her, she contrived triumphantly to carry out of the shop, as she carried it in, her air of listless indifference to everything around her. She submitted to have one hat tried on after another, an occupation in which she usually delighted.

Whether they suited her ill or well, not a sign of interest did she give, and she allowed her husband to choose her headgear for her as he had chosen the mantle.

Nothing daunted by her malice, Sir Robert took her to the best boot-shop in London, and finally to a jeweller's, where he chose a beautiful pendant of diamonds, pearls and emeralds, her favourite combination of gems.

Lady Sarah preserved the same stolidity, the same indifference throughout, and when they took their places in the train to return to Dourville, she did not even take the trouble to pick up one of her parcels when it fell on the floor.

It was a trial of strength between them; Sir Robert, on his side, still hoped against hope that his generosity would conquer her gratitude in the end, and that she would appreciate the nobility of his revenge upon a wife who had been caught in the act of attempting to desert him. Lady Sarah, on her side, determined to show him that she was not to be bought over by his kindness, fought sullenly for the maintenance of her stolid ill-temper, and succeeded so far, but failed in her amiable wish to excite her husband to ill-humour or to reproach.

When they reached the Mill-house, they got out of the carriage, which had been sent to meet them, in just the same manner as they had got in that morning. Lady Sarah cold, listless, languid, almost plain in her ill-humour; Sir Robert calm, firm, unruffled as ever.

She did not even turn to speak about the parcels which were in the carriage. As a rule she was too much excited about any new purchase even to allow the servants to bring it in for her. Seizing it with both hands, she would run to the nearest sympathiser of her own sex, Minnie, or Rhoda, or even Mrs. Hawkes, to show her new possession with the glee of a child.

Now she marched into the house as if such frivolities were altogether beneath her.

She went upstairs to dress for dinner, and came down looking rather more contented than she had done all day.

Sir Robert flattered himself that she had at last broken down under the influence of the sable cloak or the handsome pendant. But he noted, with a slight uneasiness, that in proportion as she was more satisfied, the faces of Rhoda and Minnie were graver and more disturbed.

"Well, Sarah, have you shown the girls your pretty things?" asked Sir Robert as they all took their seats at the table.

Rhoda and Minnie looked at each other uncomfortably. The baronet glanced from one to the other, and then turned to his wife, upon whose face there was a most disagreeable look of gratified malice.

"Oh, yes, they've seen the things," she said coolly. "As I don't want another cloak, I offered it to Minnie, but she thought it was too old for her; and I offered Miss Pembury the pendant, as I hate pendants myself and I thought she might like it. But she didn't care to accept it either. So I sent the cloak and the pendant, and the hats up to the Priory, in case Aileen or Philippa may like them."

There was a long silence. Sir Robert went on eating his soup without gratifying her malice by so much as a look. The other two ladies followed his example, with scalding tears in their eyes. They all waited for the explosion which, they all felt sure, must come at last, after such a shocking exhibition of ingratitude and insolence on the part of his unworthy wife.

But, while all had their eyes cast down, Sir Robert's voice, grave, quiet, apparently wholly unaffected by what had passed, broke the awkward silence.

"And Miss Pembury," he said, "I have some news that will interest you, I think. I saw, in a shop in Piccadilly, the companion print to my 'Farmer's Daughter.'"

Rhoda and Minnie looked up, smiling and admiring his courage.

Lady Sarah was defeated. Her lip trembled, and she had the grace to look ashamed of herself, as she began nervously to play with her bread.

CHAPTER XVIII.

THE COMPANION'S ORDEAL

IT was a relief to them all when Sir Robert made an excuse of urgent letters to write and bid the ladies good-night immediately after dinner, but on the other hand, Minnie and Rhoda felt very uncomfortable at the prospect of spending the evening in the society of Lady Sarah.

As it turned out, however, things went off better than they had expected. No sooner was Lady Sarah out of her husband's sight than her spirits returned, and she had the effrontery to say to Rhoda, in a low voice, when Minnie was at the other end of the drawing-room:

"You see how useless it is for you good people to make plots and plans for bad ones like me, don't you?"

Rhoda could not restrain her indignation:

"It is shocking, Lady Sarah, that you should treat your husband so, for no fault but his being too forgiving."

Lady Sarah looked frankly and boldly into her eyes.

"Forgiving! What has he to forgive?" she asked, as if in all innocence.

Rhoda was so much astonished at this retort that it was some moments before she could reply. When she had collected her thoughts, she said straightforwardly:

"You tried to run away. And he has forgiven that."

"Well, it was his wish that I should stay, wasn't it? Then he is right to be glad. It is I who am sorry, for I wanted to go."

The coolness with which she spoke frightened Rhoda for a moment. But then the absurdity of the situation suddenly struck her, after her realisation of its tragedy, and she could scarcely help laughing.

"It's of no use to argue with you, Lady Sarah," she said with a sigh.

"Not the least in the world. You see, too, that I'm in the right. Sir Robert, for what reason I don't know, wants to keep me here against my will, wants to travel with me, when he knows he'll hate it as much as I shall. Well, he has succeeded in getting his own way, and I haven't got mine. Why am I expected to be grateful then? It is he who ought to be grateful. But it is silly of him to show his gratitude by insisting upon buying me a lot of things I don't want."

Rhoda said no more, and Lady Sarah, thankful at any rate to be freed from the society of her husband, condescended to be very charming for the rest of the evening.

But there was now a new feature in her conduct which filled every one with dismay. She was civil to every one, lively and bright with Minnie and even with Rhoda, but towards Sir Robert she now maintained a demeanour of cold reserve which was disconcerting in the extreme.

It was in vain that he tried every means in his power to please her, consulted her about their travelling arrangements, asked her whether she wanted money. Even that last inducement to break down her sullen resentment failed.

She shrugged her shoulders, and without looking up, told him that, after the fuss he had made about giving her money, she had resolved not to trouble him for more than her allowance in future.

Sir Robert, greatly distressed by this new attitude, had recourse, much against his will, to his wife's parents for help in the emergency.

The Marquis was unsympathetic. He was of opinion that every man should know how to manage his own wife, and that his son-in-law had better not carry his domestic troubles outside his own door.

But Lady Eridge, who perhaps understood, better than did the Marquis, the wayward and difficult temper of their child, was greatly distressed, and did not dare to confess what Lady Sarah had told her since the frustrated elopement, news of which she had herself brought to her mother.

Lady Sarah had told her mother frankly that she hated her husband, that she would never get on any better with him than she was now doing, and that, if he were to insist upon taking her away with him to Egypt, she would throw herself into the sea on the way out.

How was Lady Eridge to tell her son-in-law this? Knowing as she did, that some of the blame for the ill-assorted marriage lay on her shoulders, she was desperately anxious to make the best of things, and the advice she at length gave Sir Robert was that he should give up the idea of Egypt, and let Lady Sarah go to the Riviera as usual without him.

"She will be with me," urged the Marchioness. "And you can trust me to look after her."

"But will you be able to prevent her seeing Jack Rotherfield?"

"Would it even be wise to do so?" urged Lady Eridge.

"What! After the other night!"

"Yes. I don't think she would ever have agreed to run away but for the discovery about the picture. Of course that was shocking, inexcusable, horrible. But I think it was more out of revenge upon you for thwarting her that she acted than from any real wish to rob you, and it's a great pity she was driven to bay over it."

"There was no help for it," said Sir Robert.

"Well, I suppose not. But, as I say, it was a pity. She is a very difficult person to manage, and of course it puts a great humiliation upon her."

"To be found out? Yes, of course. However, I can't consent to her going to the Riviera, unless, indeed, she cares to let me accompany her. My object in coming to you to-day was to find out whether you can persuade her to behave reasonably. She must not travel again without me, of that I am determined. But I should wish to leave it to you to settle with her whether she would rather spend the winter here in Dourville or abroad. In any case she has to put up with the infliction of my presence."

Lady Eridge sighed.

"Robert, I am very sorry for you," she said. "I don't quite know what to advise. But if I were you, I would shorten the period of keeping Jack away as much as possible. I don't believe there would have been any harm done but for that strong action of yours in forbidding her to speak to him. Of course that made her resentful at once."

Sir Robert, however, looked dubious.

"I thought, as you do, that there was no harm in their flirtation," he said, "and, as you know, I have given her every indulgence. But when she prefers to run away from her home to refraining from compromising correspondence, what is one to think?"

"Think anything but the worst, and you will be right. She is fond of Jack, in her superficial way, but I don't think it is fondness for him, so much as resentment against you, that made her want to run away."

"But, in Heaven's name what has she got to resent?"

"Nothing. But she always was unreasonable, and she will be to the end. Robert, take my advice. Let her go away with me, and I'll undertake to look after her."

"I must think it over," said the baronet stiffly, as he rose to go.

Hurt as he was by his wife's hard and unnatural conduct, and by the barrier she set up between them, he was determined to make one last effort that night to bring her to a more reasonable frame of mind. He was conscious that he had been guilty of no one fault in his conduct towards her except in the weakness which had caused him to be over-indulgent to her caprices.

Deep as his love for her had been, founded on admiration which had never grown weaker, the manner in which she had treated him of late had affected his own feeling for her strongly. He had known and made allowance for the difference between their temperaments, but he had always believed, in spite of her caprices and her neglect of her domestic duties, that what heart she had was sound. Now, however, he was faced with doubts which it was impossible to dispel, and it was without so much indulgence in his heart as usual that he prepared for a final battle with her.

If she were to persist in refusing to treat him with any appearance of ordinary civility, he would put it to her that some settlement would have to be arrived at to make life for either of them possible.

He feared that she would welcome the prospect, but he hoped that an appeal to her feelings might result in softening her.

In the meantime Rhoda was undergoing a painful ordeal. It was now a week since the night of the frustrated elopement, and things were going on in the same uncomfortable manner as ever at the Mill-house.

Rhoda gave most of her time to Caryl, and saw as little of either Sir Robert or Lady Sarah as could be helped, in order that nothing in her conduct might give the wife an excuse for saying that she stood between her and her husband.

Rhoda, who always did her own shopping in the evening when Caryl was in bed, was returning at dusk to the house when a man in a motor-coat came quickly across the road towards her.

She would have hurried on, for she recognised Jack Rotherfield, but he was determined to speak to her, and she had to submit. She quailed under the look of intense mistrust and dislike which shot out of his handsome dark eyes as he spoke to her.

"Miss Pembury," he said in a low voice, "I want to speak to you. You have been poisoning people's minds against me, and I have a right to be heard."

Rhoda was indignant. His manner was threatening and his tone almost abusive. And yet this was the man who had murdered Langton, who had deceived his old friend and guardian, and who had done his best to rob him of his wife.

"I will hear whatever you have to say, Mr. Rotherfield," said she.

He walked beside her, and went on in the same offended tone:

"What is it you have said against me?"

She stopped. It was now so dark that, in the side road into which they had turned, they could stand and talk without much fear of being remarked upon by passers-by.

"I have said nothing against you."

"You used a threat. You told Lady Sarah that you would tell Sir Robert something about me unless she gave up her intention of coming outside the gate to speak to me."

Rhoda was silent. She was frightened by Jack Rotherfield's manner, and would have avoided this interview had she been able to do so. But as he insisted, she thought she had better hear all that he had to say, once for all. Perhaps, also, she might be able to say something to him which would induce him to fall in with Sir Robert's wishes.

"Well," he said. "What was it you had to tell Sir Robert?"

She hesitated only a moment longer, and then replied boldly:

"You know what it was."

"I swear I haven't the least idea."

She turned quickly as if to make her escape.

But he stopped her, laying his hand lightly on her arm.

"Don't go yet, please. I must know what it is you intend to tell Sir Robert about me."

She hesitated. Then, perhaps, in the hope that he might, after all, be able to clear himself of the worst part of the guilt which she believed to weigh upon him, she said:

"I know that it was you who killed the butler, Langton."

He stood firm and did not flinch.

"Indeed! And how do you know it?"

"I saw you come out of the drawing-room and go upstairs."

"Where were you?"

"In the hall, in the corner by the tall clock."

For a moment he was silent. She stole a glance at him, and was chilled by the look upon his face. If she had until that moment believed him incapable of murder, she would have altered her opinion after seeing that look.

"And you are kind enough to take it for granted, because you imagine you saw me go upstairs, that it was I who killed the man?"

"Well, it is for others to say that. All I should say is what I saw and what I know."

"And that is next to nothing. If you had seen me strike the man you might have had something to tell. As it is——"

"As it is, I know that you were in the drawing-room with him; I heard you; and I know you went upstairs afterwards, because I saw you. If nothing happened while you were in the drawing-room, why have you never confessed that you were there?"

He hesitated and then spoke quickly:

"I'll tell you all about it, and you shall judge whether I could speak. I was in love with Lady Sarah, as you know, of course. I was rash enough, foolish enough, to leave the Mill-house, where I was staying with Sir Robert, who was then my guardian, and to go to the Priory, late at night, to see her for a few minutes, she inside and I outside the library window. Langton, the butler, knew of this; he had caught me at it before. He lay in wait for me, and when I let myself in by the drawing-room window, which I had left unfastened, I found him inside. He insulted me; I was hot-tempered then, and I knocked him down. I didn't mean to hurt him seriously, of course. That's the truth."

"It's not all the truth," said Rhoda. "His hand was cut—and so was yours. You must have used a knife."

"He struck at me with one, and I had to defend myself," said Jack.

"Why didn't you tell the whole story, if you had no intention of killing him?"

"How could I? I should have had to drag Lady Sarah's name into the business, and Sir Robert would not have married her. There was no harm in our little *tête-à-têtes*, but still it would not have done to own to them. Now would it?"

"I suppose not," said Rhoda slowly. "But it was shocking that you should have begun so soon to deceive Sir Robert. It was dreadful, terrible."

"Do you think it would serve any useful purpose to let him know all the truth now?"

"It may be necessary," said Rhoda boldly.

"And you really mean to do it?"

"I would only do it if Lady Sarah were to deceive her husband again."

Jack's face grew dark with rage; she saw his features twitching.

"What good would it do?"

"An investigation would be made, and justice would be done."

He knew what she meant. She was trembling as she spoke, but she was determined that he should know that upon his good behaviour depended his own safety. If he would keep away from the house, and refrain from communicating with Lady Sarah, she would keep silence. If he failed to do so, then she would denounce him, and he would have to stand his trial.

He understood the position perfectly; she saw this, and that there was no need to "rub it in." For a few moments he stood quietly considering the matter, and then he seemed to pull himself together, and suddenly bent forward to speak in a low voice:

"You think you are acting for the best, I've no doubt," said he. "But you are forging a chain which will hold Sir Robert as well as his wife prisoner for the rest of his life."

"No, no," said Rhoda.

She had got away. But he followed her.

"And look here," said he, as he bent down with a sudden burst of passion. "You are acting, not from good motives, but from bad ones. You want to boss the show at the Mill-house. But you won't. You have done the worst thing you could for everybody, and you mustn't expect to escape punishment. If you betray me—us, you'll repent it."

"Very well," said Rhoda. "That's my affair."

"You won't be warned?"

She would not answer him. Breaking away, she ran out into the high road, where he did not dare to follow her, and returned with rapid steps to the Mill-house.

She got back in time to dress hurriedly for dinner, and scrambled down, very pale and nervous, just as the rest were seated.

Lady Sarah looked curiously at her from time to time across the table, and Rhoda, anxious to escape an interview, ran upstairs as soon as dinner was over.

Ten minutes later, the report of a firearm, and then the agonised shriek of a woman, rang through the house.

Sir Robert rushed from his study into the hall, where he met a frightened housekeeper on the stairs.

"What was that noise?" asked he quickly. "And where did it come from?"

Mrs. Hawkes replied in a trembling voice, as she hurried upstairs,

"It sounds like a shot, sir, and it comes from Miss Pembury's room."

CHAPTER XIX.
OTHERWISE THAN INTENDED

SCARCELY had the housekeeper given this answer to her master's inquiry, when a loud knocking at the front door, and the long tinkling of the electric bell, announced that some one was there, some one, as they all guessed, who was acquainted with what had happened.

There was something so startling in this thundering at the door at the very moment when they were on their way upstairs towards the room which they imagined to be the scene of a tragedy, that both Sir Robert and Mrs. Hawkes stopped and turned upon the staircase.

"Who's that?" hissed the housekeeper.

A man-servant had run to the door, but Sir Robert turned once more and pointed imperiously upwards.

"Go on, go on, or let me pass," he said.

And then, as if the knocking at the door had been only the result of their own imaginations, excited by their fears, they both hurried on up the stairs.

Swiftly there passed through the minds of both a succession of terrible thoughts, born of the events of the past month. The housekeeper was as well aware as her master and mistress themselves that there was acute tension between them, and in all the anxiety and suspense which the whole household had endured since the thefts from the gallery had become known and whispered about, the chief hope of everybody that some sort of satisfactory way out of the family difficulties might be found, centred on Rhoda Pembury.

With her quiet manners, her attachment to the invalid boy, her evident efforts to preserve the peace between husband and wife, the girl had endeared herself to the lower members of the household as well as to Caryl, and Mrs. Hawkes in particular had persisted in believing that she would end by finding means to bring the ill-assorted couple together.

But now the housekeeper was filled with fear that the peace-maker had been the victim of a fresh tragedy.

She was even vaguely suspicious as to the hand by which such a tragedy as she feared might have been brought about. It was inevitable that some inkling of the truth about the death of poor Langton should have trickled through to the servants' hall during those ten years which had elapsed since the death of the butler, that gossip should have fixed upon Jack Rotherfield as the possible holder of the clue to that old mystery.

Now, therefore, it was not surprising that Mrs. Hawkes should ask herself whether Jack Rotherfield, who had already the guilt of one outrage at his door, might not have committed another. If Rhoda Pembury had been murdered because she stood between Lady Sarah and her husband's rival, who but that rival could have been guilty of the act?

So thought Mrs. Hawkes as she hurried along the corridor to the door of Rhoda's room.

Bursting it open without knocking, so sure was she that the sounds she had heard proceeded from this room, the housekeeper found herself in darkness. The electric light had not been turned on. The window was open, the curtains were drawn back, and a little light came from the moon, not long risen.

For a moment Mrs. Hawkes saw nothing. Then, her eyes becoming accustomed to the gloom, she perceived that there was something on the floor close by the window, something that did not move, did not utter a sound.

She moved forward quickly, and knelt down on the floor. Then a shudder went through her, and she sat back with a low cry.

Once more bending down, she raised the inert mass from the floor, turned the limp head, stared down into the ghastly face.

For a moment sight and sense seemed to fail her, and then she was roused by sounds of voices and footsteps outside the door.

Scrambling quickly to her feet, the housekeeper hurried across the floor, just as a loud knock sounded on the door of the room.

She heard the rattling of the handle and quickly turned the key in the lock at the sound of master's voice.

"Mrs. Hawkes, can I speak to you? Can you come out?"

She tried to recover her natural voice, as she answered quickly:

"In one moment, Sir Robert. Will you send for a doctor at once?"

"A doctor!" The voice was that of Jack Rotherfield.

"What has happened?" This was in Sir Robert's voice.

There was a pause, during which Mrs. Hawkes heard other voices in a confused buzz.

"There has been an accident. A bad accident, I'm afraid."

"Yes, yes. An accident. But I was the cause of it. I did it. Oh, God, let me come in, let me in."

These words were uttered in the strong voice of Jack Rotherfield, and at the same moment there came a terrific lunge against the door, which he was trying to break open.

The stern voice of Sir Robert, remonstrating, had the desired effect of making the young man desist, and then the housekeeper heard her master giving orders to one of the men-servants to go at once for a doctor.

In the meantime Mrs. Hawkes had hurriedly recrossed the floor to the window, and made one more examination of the body of the woman lying in a heap on the rug under the window.

Then the voice of Jack Rotherfield sounded loud and clear above all the others outside.

"She's dead, I know she's dead."

"Hush!"

It was Minnie who was trying to silence him, but the young man still ejaculated, in a tone of passionate remorse and horror,

"I know she's dead. I know it. It was I killed her."

"What!"

Sir Robert hissed out the word, in horror and dismay.

Jack Rotherfield went on, in a deathlike silence which made every word ring out:

"I meant only to frighten her. It was an accident. I fired a revolver into the air, as I thought, but the bullet struck her as she leaned out of the window."

There were sounds of sobbing and suppressed screaming, and in the midst of it Sir Robert knocked again at the door.

"You had better let me come in."

The housekeeper turned the key in the lock, and opened the door.

At the same moment a figure came flying along the corridor from Caryl's room, and Rhoda Pembury, pale and alarmed, joined the little group of three persons: Sir Robert, Jack Rotherfield, and Mrs. Hawkes.

"What is it? What has happened?" cried the girl. "What is all the noise?"

Sir Robert fell back, reeling.

"Thank God!" he said hoarsely, under his breath, as he looked at her.

She stared at him, trembling, then at Jack Rotherfield, who was striving to get past Mrs. Hawkes; and at the housekeeper, who held him fast by the arm.

The housekeeper suddenly relaxed her hold of Jack and beckoned to Rhoda.

"Come in with me," she said.

Rhoda staggered back.

"What is it? In my room?" stammered she.

The housekeeper nodded.

"Lady Sarah," she whispered. "She is—" And with her lips she formed the word "dead."

Both Sir Robert and Rhoda understood, and in silence they both entered the room, where Mrs. Hawkes turned up the light.

There, under the window, in her light satin dress, with the jewels round her neck and on her hands, the flowers still pinned to her bodice, her beautiful dark hair disordered by her fall, lay Lady Sarah, inert, lifeless.

A little dark stain on her satin bodice showed where the blood had oozed through from the wound in her breast.

Jack Rotherfield burst into the group and threw himself on the ground beside the dead woman. Unprincipled as he was, guilty as he was, not one of the three persons present could fail to be moved by the anguish in his face. Solemn as the moment was, and deeply as they were all impressed by the swiftness of the unexpected and as yet imperfectly understood tragedy, not one of those three, Sir Robert, Rhoda, or Mrs. Hawkes, showed half the despair which convulsed the features of the young man.

He was mad with grief. He babbled out words to which they would all fain have shut their ears; he took the lifeless hands and pressed them within his own, staring down at the dead face, calling to her, now loudly, now softly, in a way which wrung all their hearts.

The group broke up on the arrival of the doctor, and only Mrs. Hawkes and Sir Robert remained in the room while he made his brief examination.

There had never been the least doubt about the result of it. Lady Sarah had been shot through the heart, and must have died instantaneously.

Jack Rotherfield made no secret of the fact that he had been the cause of her death, but it soon leaked out that, while he declared that he had accidentally shot the lady, while intending only to attract her attention and to frighten her, he had believed, as he did so, that the woman he was frightening was Rhoda Pembury.

It was Lady Sarah's scream which had acquainted him with the fact that the bullet had struck the wrong woman.

His explanations, rambling and confused, deceived no one. All his hearers knew that he must have been on the watch for Rhoda's appearance at the window of her room, where it was often her habit to sit looking out at the water that ran through the grounds. The room being unlighted, the moment he saw a woman's figure at the window, Jack had jumped to the conclusion that it was that of Rhoda Pembury, and he had shot her, by his own account accidentally, but none the less effectually.

He was suffered to leave the house without molestation, and indeed it was necessary to suggest his withdrawal, so anxious was he to remain in the vicinity of the dead woman to whom, it could not be doubted, he had been deeply attached.

It was the doctor who got rid of him, and who then turned his attention to Rhoda, upon whom the tragic event, which she understood better than any one, had had an overwhelming effect.

For a short time she lay prostrate, absolutely overcome by the knowledge that it was in mistake for herself that Jack Rotherfield had shot Lady Sarah. Rhoda remembered the glances which the unfortunate lady had thrown repeatedly in her direction during dinner, and did not doubt that Lady Sarah had gone to the room of her boy's companion in order to speak to her privately. There seated or standing at the window, in the half darkness, she had been mistaken by Jack Rotherfield for Rhoda, and, although his statement was to the effect that his intention had only been to attract her attention or to frighten her—for he had given both explanations—Rhoda was quite sure that he had intended to shoot her, in revenge for what she had done in keeping him apart from Lady Sarah, or to prevent any indiscretions on her part in the shape of revelations concerning the death of Langton.

Suddenly Rhoda raised herself from the couch in Lady Sarah's boudoir where she had been placed.

"Caryl!" she whispered.

Mrs. Hawkes, having superintended the carrying of the body of poor Lady Sarah into her own bedroom, had left Sir Robert alone with the dead lady and had given her attention to Rhoda.

Rhoda had caught the faint sound of the boy's voice, through the open doors. He was calling for her.

"I must go to him." She struggled to her feet, and turning unsteadily, said: "Mrs. Hawkes, will you send word to the Priory of what has happened? And ask whether Lady Eridge will come? She will have to take Caryl away."

"Yes. Quite right. I hadn't thought of it."

Rhoda went slowly to the boy's room and found him crying in his little bed. His nurse was with him, doing her best to soothe him, but rumours of the tragedy which had killed his mother had already reached his ears, and he would not be comforted without his friend.

"Rhoda, Rhoda," cried he, as she came in, looking very white, "Is it true? Is mama dead?"

"Oh, they shouldn't have told you!"

"But I guessed." She was beside him by this time, and his arm was round her neck. "You remember that evening when she was kind, and kissed me, and cried? I knew that meant something was going to happen, and I've wondered and wondered what it was. Now I know."

Rhoda wiped away her own tears. He drew her head down to his level.

"Poor mama. I'm sorry. She was so pretty!" There was a pause, while Rhoda acquiesced, sobbing. Then he said quickly: "But you will stay with me, won't you?"

Rhoda did not know what to say.

"Your grandmama will want to take care of you, Caryl, I think," she said. "She will be very, very kind, and so will your aunts, I'm sure."

"Yes, they're all kind, but I want *you*. Will you promise to stay with me?"

"I can't promise anything yet. You must wait, and be sure we will take good care of you, Caryl," said the girl, who could scarcely speak.

The wrench of the tragedy had been great: that of parting with Caryl would, she felt, be greater still. Yet how was it to be avoided?

Within half an hour the marchioness arrived with Lady Aileen; and both, after a long and distressing interview with Sir Robert, came with him into Caryl's room.

At once Rhoda noticed, with deep distress, that there was a difference in his manner to herself.

Instead of being merely sad and grave, Sir Robert, when he turned towards her, was distant, formal, stern and cold. She was cut to the heart, and understood that he looked upon her as in part the cause of the death of his wife.

True though this was, in a sense, yet as Rhoda was wholly innocent in the matter, she felt that it was an injustice that she should be treated in this manner.

In the circumstances, it was, of course, impossible either to explain or to accuse. She could only submit, and suffer.

Before many minutes were over, however, she had something to think about which distracted her thoughts, for the time, from Sir Robert and his unkindness.

Lady Eridge, deeply distressed as she was at her daughter's sudden and tragic death, seemed to feel something not unlike a sense of relief that her troubles on behalf of the erratic and self-willed Lady Sarah were at an end.

"What are you going to do, Miss Pembury?" she asked in a low voice, as she bent over the boy.

"She is going to stay with me," cried Caryl, as he joined his hands together round Rhoda's neck, and clinging to her, refused to relax his hold.

Lady Eridge looked at her.

"You can't stay here, of course?"

"Of course not. I am going away at once," said Rhoda.

The boy burst into loud sobs.

The marchioness bent down to whisper in her ear.

"I'm going to take him to the Priory, to-night, out of the way of everything. His father will not mind, I'm sure."

"No. That will be the best thing possible."

"Will you come with him?"

"Oh, to the Priory? I think I'd rather not. You see I feel so miserable, and as if I were guilty of—of——"

"Hush! That is absurd. If you come with us, there will be no question that it will be best for you as well as for Caryl. And it will show that her people understand. Now will you come?"

Still feeling as if she were held guilty by the boy's father, Rhoda glanced towards him.

"If Sir Robert agrees, I'll go," said she.

The marchioness went over to him and they exchanged a few words. Then Lady Eridge came back.

"He agrees with me that nothing could be better. And he thinks that you had better both come at once. Of course you had better be near at hand, for there will be questions to answer, since the terrible affair happened in your room. And you will be near enough at the Priory."

It was settled at once. Within an hour little Caryl had been removed to his couch on wheels, and wrapped up carefully, was on his way to the Priory, in the company of Rhoda, his grandmother, and one of his aunts.

Rhoda took care not to meet Sir Robert before leaving the house. She could not face those cold looks of his again. And it was with a very heavy heart, and a sense that, in spite of her utmost efforts, she had lost a dear friend, that she left the Mill-house for a second time.

CHAPTER XX AND LAST.
SIR ROBERT'S SECRET

SAFELY housed at the Priory, Rhoda escaped much of the terrible anxiety and distress which reigned at the Mill-house during the next few days.

There was an inquest, but Rhoda happily escaped once more the trial of being called as a witness. Her health had broken down under the strain of the past few weeks, and although she was allowed to see Caryl for a little while every day, she was kept very quiet and received no visits, even from her own people.

The ladies at the Priory were, however, very kind to her, and did their best to make her forget what she had gone through.

Nobody knew better than they what she must have suffered at the hands of the exacting and capricious Lady Sarah, who, with all her charm, had been a difficult person to live with.

At the inquest Jack Rotherfield was called as a witness, and he was either lucky enough or clever enough to disarm every one by the depth of his distress at what he had done.

He declared that, having had a little quarrel with Sir Robert recently, he had been shy of coming to the house, but that, having met Miss Pembury one day out of doors, he had been anxious for her to come out and speak to him again, as he wished her to make his peace with Sir Robert.

Not being able to attract her attention in any other way, he had on seeing Miss Pembury, as he supposed, at her window, fired a revolver which he always carried about with him; and to his horror, a scream had told him that the bullet had struck the lady whom he had until that moment believed to be Miss Pembury, but who he then discovered by the voice to be Lady Sarah.

The story was not at all a probable one, but Jack was in such a state of acute distress that he produced a favourable impression, and he was let off lightly in examination and re-examination by the coroner and jury.

Sir Robert was able to testify to the truth of the statement that there had been a little quarrel between him and Rotherfield, and to the certainty he felt that Jack would not willingly have injured Lady Sarah.

The verdict brought in by the jury was one of death by misadventure, and the threatened scandal was happily averted.

There was a good deal of gossip, there were rumours, there were whispers, but no arrest was made, and the affair was hushed up, though not without some trembling on the part of the families involved.

Autumn being now well advanced, there was a discussion as to what should become of the usual holiday at the Riviera, and in the end it was abandoned by Lady Eridge, who decided to remain at the Priory.

There Caryl was to stay also, and Lady Eridge told Rhoda that she had questioned Sir Robert about his plans, and that he had decided to shut up the Mill-house and to go abroad.

"I then suggested," went on the marchioness, "that we should ask you to stay with Caryl, and Sir Robert agreed. But really he seems to take no interest in anything since the death of his wife."

Rhoda was quite ready to fall in with this arrangement, and she hoped that, before going away, the baronet would, on saying good-bye, show her once more a little of his old kindness. For the remembrance of his cold looks and harsh voice when he spoke to her on the night of Lady Sarah's death had made a wound which did not heal.

To her bitter disappointment, she was told one evening, when she returned to the Priory after a walk into the town by herself, that Sir Robert had called in her absence, had said good-bye to his boy, and that he would start for Egypt that very evening.

Rhoda shed hot tears at the thought that he had gone away without one word to her. She had revered him so long, had sympathised with him, done her best to keep the difficult household going during the lifetime of his wife, that she felt deeply hurt at this lack of ordinary kindness which she had had a right to expect.

It prepared her for a future in which she would find herself cut off altogether from the Mill-house and its inmates; for she did not doubt that, when he returned in the spring, Sir Robert would send for his son, and she would then get her dismissal.

Rhoda felt that Lady Eridge understood something of her feelings, for the marchioness was very kind to her, and did her best to prove that her services were appreciated.

Perhaps Caryl, young as he was, understood too that Rhoda had not been treated quite well, for he said nothing to her about the farewell interview with his father.

The winter passed quickly for all that. Rhoda and Caryl became so devoted to each other that the thought of a possible parting, which was ever present to the woman and which often occurred to the child, grew more and more painful.

But at Christmas time there occurred one incident which afforded Rhoda for the time a little consolation.

It was a visit from Jack Rotherfield.

He arrived at the Priory one afternoon just after luncheon, and had a long interview with Lady Eridge in the drawing-room, at the end of which the marchioness sent for Rhoda. The marchioness rose from her chair, and, advancing towards the girl, who uttered an exclamation of horror on seeing who the visitor was, said in her ear, "He has behaved well to us, and he wishes to make some sort of apology to you."

And with these words the marchioness left them together.

Jack, who was looking thin and ill, came frankly towards Rhoda. He did not attempt to shake hands:

"I suppose you are surprised to see me, Miss Pembury," he said. "But as Lady Eridge sent for me to explain certain stories about poor Lady Sarah and me, which had come to her ears, I thought I should like to see you and to ask your forgiveness for my share in making you lose your home at the Mill-house."

Rhoda was not ready with an answer, and she murmured some indistinct and rather cold words of acknowledgment.

"I know you did your best for her," he said frankly; "and that you were perfectly right in doing what I so much resented. All the same, she would never have been happy with Sir Robert. And you know it. She irritated him, and she got on his nerves. They were an ill-matched pair from the first."

"Why have you come?" asked Rhoda abruptly.

"Lady Eridge sent for me, as I told you. She had heard about those interviews poor Lady Sarah and I had before she was married. I told her everything. And I wanted to thank you for holding your tongue. You might have done for me altogether if you had appeared at the inquest, or if you had talked afterwards. I beg your pardon with all my heart for any harm I have ever done you, or for any I, in my mad rage, may have wished to do you."

Rhoda could not but think that this frankness in a man of his character came perilously near to effrontery. But she was not inclined to stir up the ashes of dead resentments, and she told him that, if Sir Robert could forgive him, she would not hold back.

"I am writing to him to-night," said Jack.

The interview was not very long, but when it was over and Jack Rotherfield had gone away, she fell to wondering what he would say about her in his letter to Sir Robert.

Her heart was still very sore about the departure of the baronet without a word of farewell to her, and she felt that he still associated her unfairly in his mind with all his misfortunes.

It was true, indeed, that she had always been at the Mill-house when they happened.

As the winter went on, Caryl, who received frequent letters from his father, without one word in them of Rhoda, became more and more disturbed as to his future.

He dictated his letters to Rhoda, who transcribed them for him; but, although they both knew that the baronet must recognise her handwriting, there was never any message in Sir Robert's letters to his son, to any one except the ladies of the marquis's family, and the head servants at the Mill-house.

These two, Rhoda and Caryl, began to talk about what they should do when the spring came, and the boy told her he intended to ask his father to let him go abroad with her, if she would not come back to the Mill-house with him.

And so the weeks rolled by until winter was over, and the early days of April found Caryl still at the Priory in the care of Rhoda.

There had been a long pause since Sir Robert's last letter, and all at the Priory were rather anxious as to his movements. He had said nothing about coming home, had not answered a question put on the subject by his son, and there was much perplexity as to the cause of his silence.

It was now six months since the death of Lady Sarah, and the first horror of the event had passed away.

Rhoda had been pushing Caryl's wheeled couch about the grounds for him to admire the early spring flowers in the borders, and the daffodils among the grass on the slopes opposite to the house, and she had just taken him indoors, when the fancy seized him that he would like a bunch of daffodils to put in the big flower-vase in the old nursery which had been given up to him as a sitting-room.

Rhoda went out to get the flowers, carrying on her arm a wooden trug containing a knife to cut them with.

She had got into the winding walk that led to the grass slopes when she suddenly became aware that there was a gentleman coming towards her from the little gate that led through the plantation.

She stopped, her heart beating very fast. For it was Sir Robert Hadlow.

He stopped too, and then he came towards her.

The joy she felt on seeing that he did not mean to avoid her got into her head and rendered her so confused and excited that she was without words when he came up.

Raising his hat rather formally, as she thought, but without the cold sternness which had characterised his manner on the fatal night of Lady Sarah's death, he said:

"How do you do, Miss Pembury. I hope my unannounced arrival has not caused you any alarm. All is well, I hope, with the ladies, and with Caryl?"

"Oh, yes, they are all quite well. And Caryl, I think, is getting a little stronger. The doctor spoke very promisingly indeed only two days ago about him."

"That's excellent news. And you? Have you been well? I think, Miss Pembury, you are looking thinner."

Rhoda reddened. She was beginning to recover some of her lost self-possession.

"I am glad to be able to say that you look better, much better. I think your change must have done you a great deal of good."

"Not the least doubt about it. Next winter, if all goes well, I think I shall take Caryl with me if I go away."

"You are longing to see him. Will you go in without preparing him? or shall I tell him first?"

"Well, first I should like a little talk with you. Can you spare me five minutes?"

"Oh, yes."

She turned, and they walked in silence along the winding path, bordered on one side by a well kept hedge which was as yet only faintly green. He looked better and happier too, Rhoda thought, than he had done in the old days at the Mill-house. Certainly he had then led such a life of anxiety on account of his wife's caprices and Jack Rotherfield's escapades that domestic tranquillity was out of the question.

As the silence continued, Rhoda presently stole a glance at Sir Robert, and found that he was looking at her intently.

"You have been very unfairly treated," he said abruptly.

The blood rushed into her face.

"I have been very happy—with Caryl," she answered in a whisper.

"Yes. But while you were at the Mill-house you had to suffer a great deal, both from my wife and from me. Between the two of us the situation, for a girl, must have been almost unendurable. But for your feeling for Caryl you could not have borne it."

"That's all over now," she said in a stifled voice. "I can remember only the best part of it, your kindness, and Lady Sarah's brilliant charm."

A shadow passed over his face.

"Yes," he said solemnly. "That's what I like to recollect. The best, the brightest side." He paused and then said abruptly:

"I'm afraid I was rather brutal to you on that last night, the terrible night."

Rhoda drew a long breath.

"Brutal! Oh, no. You couldn't be that. You were cold, you even seemed hard, but it was because you were not yourself, you were—overwhelmed."

He listened in silence, and there was a pause. They still walked along the winding path, where there was just room for two, side by side.

"It wasn't exactly that," he said. "I have a confession to make, a terrible confession."

Rhoda's cheeks blanched. What was he going to say?

"You were wounded, I suppose, that I went away without saying good-bye to you, when you had been so good to my boy, so patient with my wife, so conscientious for me?"

"Oh, pray don't think about it. Of course, at such a time, after such a tragedy——"

He cut her short.

"Tragedy! Yes, it was a tragedy. Can you guess, I wonder, what a tragedy it was to me?"

"I think I can. Worshipping this lovely woman, in all her beauty and charm, the effect upon you must have been stupendous, unimaginable."

Sir Robert turned upon her suddenly, with a fire she had never before seen shining in his eyes.

"That was not the worst part of it," he said in a sonorous voice. "What I was suffering from when that awful sight was suddenly presented to my eyes was—self-reproach. Self-reproach so terrible, so keen, that I could have cut off my right hand, drowned myself, shot myself, in the depths of my own self-abasement."

Rhoda almost thought he had lost his reason, so amazing, so preposterous did such an attitude seem in the husband who had done so much for a wife who neglected and despised him.

With a pained frown he went on:

"I have felt the need of confession for a long time, ever since, in fact, and now I must make it and have done with it, once for all. The sight of her dead white face struck me dumb with anguish, with self remorse, not because I loved her, but—because I hated her."

"Oh, no, no. It's not possible. When you were so patient, so tender, so indulgent!"

He turned to her quickly:

"And that was the reason why. I was not indulgent, but over-indulgent. It was to salve my conscience, to stifle it. Heaven knows," he went on earnestly, "that I loved her passionately, desperately once. For years she was my ideal; to the last in appearance she remained my model of loveliness in a woman. But she had lost my heart long before she died. She could have kept it easily enough had she wished. But she did not wish. My affection bored her, and she killed it, killed it deliberately. Knowing that the link between us was so slender that it might at any moment snap, and wishing for Caryl's sake to keep it intact, I put up with everything, I yielded to her in everything. I made sacrifices, I gave up my own wishes to hers. But," and he turned upon her again with fire in his quiet eyes, "I

140

should not have been so indulgent, so yielding, if I had loved her. It was the tragedy of it that I had grown to hate her. When she lay dead I felt remorse, excitement, horror. But of tenderness scarcely a trace. And," he lowered his voice as if in shame, "it was because I felt as I did feel that I had to go away without seeing you, or speaking to you. I was afraid that you would find me out. It would have shocked you. You might have found out more too. So it was better that I should go as I did go."

Half-stunned, Rhoda turned and led the way back to the house.

"You must see Caryl," she said hoarsely.

She could scarcely realise the secret with which she had been entrusted. It was so hard, remembering his indulgence to his wilful wife, to understand the motive which had prompted his excess of kindness.

They went upstairs to Caryl's room, after Sir Robert had met and spoken to the ladies of the house.

The boy had seen him from his window, and was clapping his hands with glee.

"Papa, papa," cried he, "Oh, how glad, how glad I am!"

He seized his father's hand, and received his kiss, and then he held out his other hand to Rhoda.

"Come here, Rhoda, come here," cried he.

Timidly, and as it were reluctantly, she came. Caryl put her hand into that of his father, and held them together.

"Papa, you won't let her go now, will you?" he whispered.

Rhoda was crying. Sir Robert looked at her very tenderly over the little wheel-couch, and said in a low voice as he pressed her hand in his:

"No, Caryl, I won't let her go away again."